PRAI[illegible]

"*Creighton Hill* is [illegible] exciting adventure. I loved the [illegible] woven together. I look forward to the next [illegible] *Time Captives* and recommend the series to anyone, but especially to younger readers looking for a both a fun and meaningful adventure. I know I would have loved it as a child."

— Jaye L. Knight, author of *Ilyon Chronicles*

"Morgan had me hooked from the opening paragraph. Delightfully original and imaginative, *Creighton Hill* is perfect for any fan of C.S. Lewis or Wayne Thomas Batson. I can't wait to read the rest of the trilogy!"

—Ashley Elliott, author of *Becoming Nikki*

"A delightful little adventure of family and faith in an interesting new world, *Time Captives* is familiar, and yet unlike any fantasy I've read before. Where is book two???"

—Kendra E. Ardnek, author of *The Ankulen*

"This has something for everyone—laughs, adventure, mysterious disappearances, codes. You can't go wrong with *Creighton Hill*!"

—Katelyn Snell,
www.bring-your-own-books.blogspot.com

Time Captives

Creighton Hill

Morgan E Huneke
1 Cor. 1:25-28

BOOKS BY MORGAN ELIZABETH HUNEKE

MIDDLE GRADE

Across the Stars

The Experiment

Espionage: A Companion to Time Captives

Time Captives Trilogy

Book One: Creighton Hill

Book Two: The Crossways

Book Three: Crannig Castle

YOUNG ADULT

Twisted Dreams

PICTURE BOOK

Carrie Mouse and the Giant Garage

Time Captives

Creighton Hill

Morgan Elizabeth Huneke

SWP ShireWood Press

2nd edition published in June 2019
by ShireWood Press
www.shirewoodpress.com

www.morganhuneke.com

All scriptures are taken from the 1599 Geneva Bible.

ISBN: 978-1-7330462-0-6

To my mom, for believing in this book even when I didn't and always being there to help me work out the problems and listen to my complaints.

Contents

Character Guide

Time Captives

Abigail Hubbard—Time Captive from 1820

Allan Hubbard—12-year-old Time Captive from 2000. He is brother to Emily, Jill, Joey, and Anna

Bethany Hubbard—Time Captive from 1980

Calvin Hubbard—Time Captive from 1920

Eleanor Hubbard—Time Captive from 1940

Emily Hubbard—14-year-old Time Captive from 2000. Sister to Allan, Jill, Joey, and Anna

George Hubbard—Time Captive from 1800

Jill Hubbard—11-year-old Time Captive from 2000. Sister of Emily, Allan, Joey, and Anna

Joey Hubbard—10-year-old Time Captive from 2000. Brother of Emily, Allan, Jill, and Anna

Jonathan Hubbard—Time Captive from 1960

Mary Hubbard—Time Captive from 1860

Samantha Hubbard—Time Captive from 1900

Theodore Hubbard—Time Captive from 1880

Thomas Hubbard—Time Captive from 1840

Other Characters

Ammeelia—a young kalican known by Abigail. Luuke's granddaughter

Anna Hubbard—younger sister to Emily, Allan, Jill, and Joey

Camthalion—elven scholar imprisoned at Crannig Castle

Claw—a sailor on the *Black Vengeance*

Draewin—elf boy imprisoned in Calhortz, nephew of Camthalion. Brother of Havilan and Estranna

Estranna—elf girl imprisoned in Calhortz, niece of Camthalion. Sister of Havilan and Draewin

Evalin—kalican known by Abigail. Sister to Luuke

Havilan—elf imprisoned in Calhortz, nephew of Camthalion. Brother of Draewin and Estranna

Jeremy Herb—pirate captain of the *Black Vengeance*, in service to Toarna

Leela—kalican. Peetur's mother and Naythin's wife

Luuke—kalican known by Abigail. Brother to Evalin and grandfather to Ammeelia

Mudan—stryte king of Calhortz. Husband of Toarna

Naythin—kalican known by Emily, Allan, Jill, and Joey. Father of Peetur and husband of Leela

Peetur—young kalican accompanying Emily, Allan, Jill, and Joey. Son of Naythin and Leela

Ranna—maid to Toarna befriended by Abigail

Spivey—first mate of the *Black Vengeance*

Toarna—Stryte queen of Calhortz, wife of Mudan

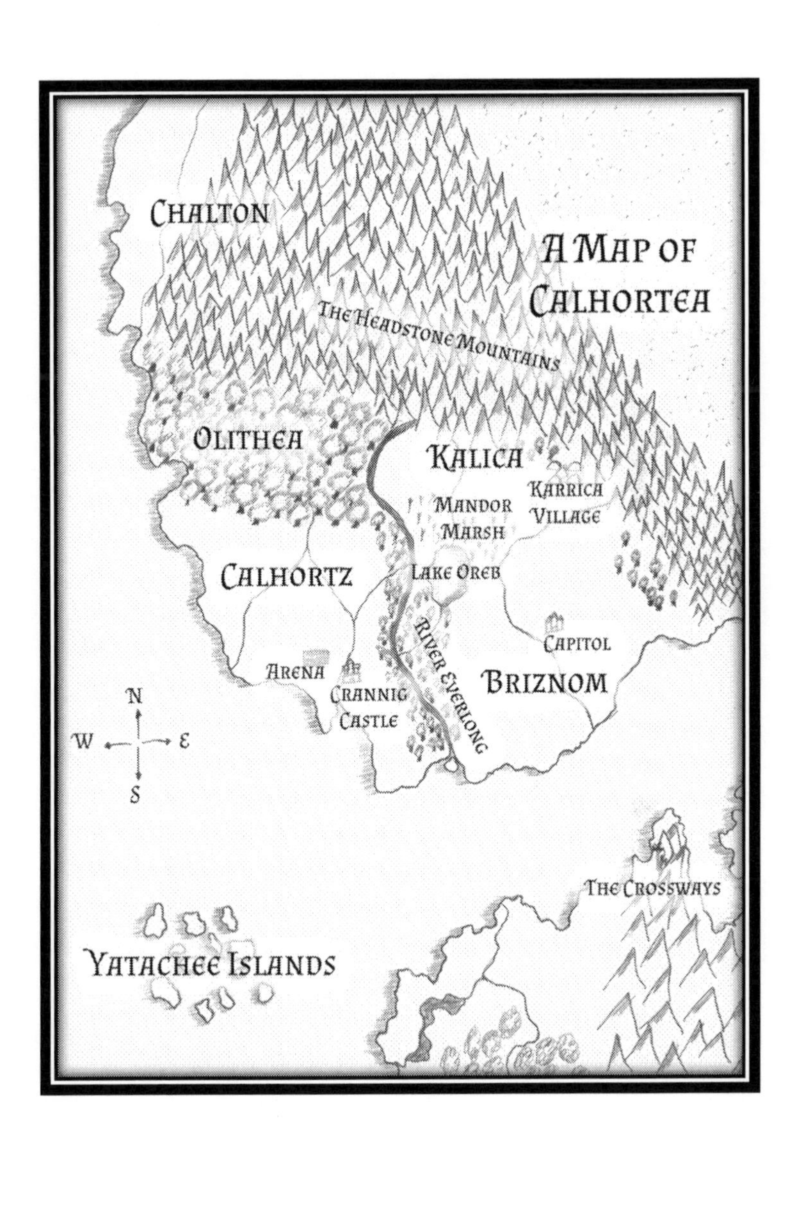
A Map of Calhortea
Chalton
The Headstone Mountains
Olithea
Kalica
Mandor Marsh
Karrica Village
Calhortz
Lake Oreb
River Everlong
Capitol
Briznom
Arena
Crannig Castle
N
W
E
S
The Crossways
Yatachee Islands

Prologue

"It was July first, 1800, the day George Hubbard disappeared. He was just a boy, twelve years old, a good lad, not one to run away. His family thought he was kidnapped, the neighbors thought he had run away to sea, the townspeople thought he had been murdered. But no one knows what really happened to George Hubbard. No trace of him was ever found. Ever since that day, every twenty years, a child twelve years of age, born a Hubbard, in this very house, has disappeared mysteriously, leaving no trace. Next time . . . next time it might be one of you!"

"Is it really true, Grampa?" a wide-eyed boy of five asked.

"Of course it is," the old man told his grandson.

"No it isn't," a very matter-of-fact seven year old girl contradicted. "You're just teasing us, Grampa, I know. No one can mysteriously disappear leaving no trace. It isn't realistic."

"You're right, Emily," her grandfather said thoughtfully. "It isn't realistic. However, a good many things happen in this world that are not realistic, things supernatural."

"Like miracles," the little boy put in.

"Yes, Allan, like miracles," Grampa agreed.

Emily shook her head. "I still don't believe it."

A girl of four climbed up on her grampa's lap. "I believe you."

"I know you do, Jillie. I know you do."

Seven Years Later

Chapter One
News

2000

Joey rubbed his sleeve across his eyes. He wasn't exactly ashamed of crying, but he was glad of the falling rain to disguise his tears. But, well, he was ten years old, and he didn't *really* want to be seen crying at that age. He glanced at his sister Jill. He would have died before he would have admitted it, but he wanted her to hug him. There were times when one just needed a big sister, and this was one of them.

He took a deep breath and looked once more toward his grampa's coffin, which sat at the graveside, ready to be buried next to his wife. Grampa hadn't been *that* old; why had he died already? Joey sniffed.

"I'm just not ready to let him go," Jill said. "Why did God have to take him away so soon?"

"Will you please keep your supernatural hogwash to yourself?" Emily complained.

Jill let out a muffled cry. Joey seethed, but there was nothing he could do. The last thing he wanted to do was start a fight at his grampa's funeral. His younger sister Anna leaned her head against his shoulder. Joey bit his lip and put his arm around her. He could pretend it was for her sake, though it was really for his own. His brother Allan was close on his other side. Only Emily stood apart, and that was fine with him.

"It's time to go home," Mom said. Only they weren't really going home, at least, not yet. They were going to Grampa's house, Creighton Hill, the family estate. Dad needed to be there to work out things dealing with Grampa's death. A house that was unbearably empty without Grampa's mischievous smile and constant storytelling.

Joey followed his siblings to the family's Suburban, and settled himself in the back seat. He stared out the window at the pouring rain. All his feistiness and sarcastic responses seemed to have drained out of him with Grampa's death.

Emily slumped in the seat in front of him. Joey couldn't tell if she was more upset at losing Grampa or having her hair plastered to her head in an unseemly fashion. He scowled at the back of her head.

Jill slipped her hand into his. For once, Joey didn't want to shrug it away.

~

Joey wandered the halls aimlessly once he had changed out of his wet clothes. He felt dejected, something he had never before experienced. He knew Grampa was in a better place, but still he didn't know what to do at Grampa's house without him.

He meandered down the stairs and found himself in Grampa's study. It smelled delightfully of old books. That was pretty much all he liked about books—too many words made his head swim. He liked his stories in a visual medium. Except when Grampa read to him. That was the only time he didn't mind the absence of visual aids.

This was stupid. Thinking about Grampa would only make things worse. Better to go pick a fight with Emily.

The door opened. "It's time for dinner."

Joey looked toward Emily. She didn't look nearly as upset as Jill had all afternoon, nor as if she were and trying to hide it.

"Aren't you sad at all that we lost Grampa?" he demanded. "Won't you miss him telling us stories and playing games with us and taking us cool places? Won't you miss him being there for us?"

"No, I won't miss his stupid stories about folks disappearing. I don't know why anyone would."

Joey scowled at her. "Don't you miss him at all?"

"He's my Grampa, of course I miss him. But don't you go making a big deal out of his stories. I don't want to mar my memories."

"You mar your own memories." He was getting irritated with Emily on purpose and it felt good.

"Go sit at the table. Wash your hands first."

Emily walked away. Just out of defiance, Joey skipped washing up. He didn't care.

Just as he sat down at the dining room table, Jill and Allan walked in. Jill took a seat between Joey and her father.

"How are you doing, Jillie?" Mr. Hubbard asked gently.

"I'm alright," she said.

"No she's not." Emily walked out of the kitchen with a plate balanced on each hand. "She's been crying all day."

"That's only natural. It's going to be very hard to get used to doing without your grampa."

"Life's been hard to you, Dad," Emily said.

"First your sister dies, then your mother, and now your father."

"Aunt Bethany didn't die," Joey jumped in. "She disappeared. Grampa said so."

Emily narrowed her eyes skeptically. "Pish posh. People don't just disappear."

"But Grampa said . . ."

"Children!" Mrs. Hubbard appeared in the doorway. "This is not the time, nor is it the place for arguing about what happened to Aunt Bethany."

Murmurs of "Yes, ma'am," trickled around the table. Mrs. Hubbard took her place at the table. The family joined hands, and Mr. Hubbard said grace. No one, not even Joey, despite his usual insatiable appetite, did much more than pick at his or her food. No one seemed to have much of an appetite. It was too hard to be there without Grampa.

"Dad," Anna asked, "when will we be going home?"

"That question has a very interesting answer, Anna," Mr. Hubbard said. "We are not going to be living at home anymore. We are going to live here."

"What?" Joey's mouth dropped open. That was ridiculous. They couldn't just move. "But what about all of our friends? Our life's there, not here."

"It's only an hour away," Mrs. Hubbard reassured him. "We won't lose touch with our friends.

And we can still attend the same church."

"Creighton Hill is closer to my work," Mr. Hubbard said. "The house is larger, as is the yard. We'll be much more comfortable here than at our current house. You won't even have to share bedrooms unless you want to. But the biggest advantage is that Creighton Hill does not have a mortgage."

"I guess that's a plus," Allan said.

"But what about Grampa's stories?" Anna protested. "What if one of us disappears?"

"Hogwash," Emily muttered.

"I admit our family does have a history of early deaths," Mr. Hubbard said, "but it has nothing to do with the house. So, Anna, there is no more need to worry about one of us 'disappearing' here than there was at home."

Emily directed her gaze toward Anna with a look reminiscent of a sneer. Joey glared at her. She shouldn't treat her younger siblings like that. Everyone was silent for a moment.

"How long until we move?" Jill asked finally.

"It will take some time to get everything legal straightened out," Mr. Hubbard said, "but we should be able to move in by the end of the month."

"I don't like being here without Grampa," Jill said.

"Neither do I, Jillie. But this house will be a good thing for our family. You'll see."

Chapter Two
Moving

JOEY PILED THE LAST OF HIS THINGS INTO A BOX. Good thing the box was big. He didn't want to have to organize it. Jill would do it if he asked, but he didn't want to ask. She was in her room with Anna and Emily, and Emily had been making nasty comments all day. Apparently, the bedrooms they had always slept in at Creighton Hill weren't good enough for her simply because they had been a nursery once upon a time.

Joey hoisted the box up on his shoulder and walked out to the Suburban. He slid it into the trunk, then paused to watch his dad and Peter Swann carry a couch out of the house. They lifted it into the moving van and turned back to the house. Joey followed.

"I'm glad we get to see you before we move away," Joey said to Peter.

Peter chuckled. "We'll still be going to church together. It's not the end of the world."

"Yeah, but kids disappear at Creighton Hill. Something could happen."

Joey looked up into the young man's face. He had always admired Peter Swann. Peter never had any disdain for younger boys, and was always encouraging to them and a good role model.

"You aren't going to disappear, Joey," Peter said. "No worries."

Joey wasn't so sure, but before he could say anything, Allan called to him from the house.

"Joey, come see if the girls need any help."

"Do I have to?" Joey complained. "Emily's in there."

"Go on," Peter encouraged.

Sighing, Joey followed his brother to the girls' room. Allan pushed the door open. The room looked strange and bare, the beds were nothing but frames, cardboard boxes were scattered randomly about.

"Jill, do you need any help carrying your things?"

"Yes, thanks, Allan. This box is ready to go out." Jill gestured to the one she had just finished taping up.

"I've got a box ready, too," Anna said.

"Emily?" Allan asked.

"No thank you," Emily responded. "I am perfectly capable of carrying my own stuff."

"Have it your way, and be glad of it," Joey said. "I don't want to carry your rotten old stuff anyway."

"Your stuff is the rotten stuff."

"No it isn't."

Emily shrugged. "Suit yourself."

"Come on, Joey," Allan said.

Allan picked up Jill's box, and Joey grabbed Anna's.

"You really shouldn't agitate Emily," Allan said on the way out to the moving van. "It only makes things worse."

"I don't care if they're worse," Joey huffed. "Emily shouldn't be so mean."

"I'm just saying it isn't her fault alone the two of you argue."

"Never said it was."

"Joey." Allan's tone held a warning.

Joey sighed. He didn't know how Allan and Jill could be so good so much of the time. It wasn't natural at all for him.

Joey and Allan helped bring many more boxes out of the house, while the men carried the heavier objects. Everything went smoothly and surprisingly without event, however, it was still difficult to leave forever the place they had long called home.

"We must look a last time on our ancestral home," Jill said as they stood gazing at the house.

"Except we're going *to* our ancestral home," Joey pointed out, "even if we haven't actually lived there before, only visited."

Emily scowled. "You guys read too much."

"You don't read enough," Anna retorted. "Not the right kind of books, anyway."

"Well, at least I don't read the kind of books that make me want to stay in a nursery as a teenager," Emily returned.

"Do try not to spoil our last look at home," Jill said.

But Emily's sneering comments had already ruined it for the others.

Chapter Three

The Door at the Back of the Wardrobe

EARLY MORNING SUNLIGHT FILTERED IN THROUGH the blinds. Joey yawned and stretched, then climbed out of bed.

"Good morning, Allan."

"Good morning," Allan replied.

Joey pulled his church clothes out of the closet and hurriedly dressed. He went to the communicating door between his and Allan's room and the girls' room and peeked in.

"Are you girls up yet?"

Anna leapt out of bed. "I am now." She crossed the room to the wardrobe and began searching for a dress. Joey crept over to Jill's bed and yanked the covers off of her.

"Wake up, sleepyhead."

"I was awake, no thanks to you," Jill grumbled. She got up, wrapping a blanket around her shoulders.

"Here's your dress," Anna said as she handed Jill a dark blue cotton dress from the wardrobe. She selected a pink gingham for herself. As she closed the door, a flash of light caught Joey's attention.

"Wait a minute." Anna opened the door again at Joey's words. He came up behind them. "What's that light in there?"

Anna frowned. "I don't see anything."

"You're right, Joey," said Jill.

Joey stepped past the girls and pushed the dresses aside.

Allan came into the room buttoning up his shirt. "What are you looking at?"

"Jill and Joey see something in the wardrobe," Anna said.

"What is it?" Allan came closer. "That's weird."

"What?" Anna demanded.

"It's a spot of light," Joey said.

"But it's making words," Jill added.

The point of light lengthened and curved. Writing appeared on the back of the wardrobe. The children watched as lines became letters, and the letters became words. Jill read them aloud for Anna's benefit.

"When these words are spoken,
A land will appear."

The words shone out at them for a moment, then faded away. Allan stepped into the wardrobe. He ran his hand over the wood.

"No trace of them now," he said. "There's only a knot in the wood. Odd it wasn't sanded down."

The back of the wardrobe swung away from them. Only pitch black could be seen through the opening. Allan looked back at his siblings, then stepped inside. Anna followed.

"What's in there, Allan?" Joey stepped through the wardrobe into the secret passage, Jill close behind him. The back of the wardrobe slammed shut. Jill let out a muffled shriek.

"Maybe they all did die," Joey said in a spooky voice. He knew he shouldn't, but he couldn't help himself. "Maybe they were trapped in here, and died of starvation. Their bodies would have laid in here for decades decomposing. There could be skeletons, or half rotted corpses, just around the corner."

Jill screamed.

"What's the matter, Jill?" Allan asked.

"I touched something." Her voice quavered. "It felt like . . . a body."

Joey tried not to laugh. "That was me."

"It's okay," Allan reassured Jill. "I'm sure there's nobody in here but us. Joey, you should be ashamed of yourself for scaring the girls like that."

"Sorry."

"But there's probably mice," Anna put in.

"Jillie, are you willing to explore this passage," Allan said, "to see where it goes?"

"Only if we know we can get out again."

Joey turned back to the hidden door and felt around on the wall. "I found a latch on the door," he said after a moment. It swung open again.

Inwardly, he gave a relieved sigh at the knowledge they could get out.

"I guess I'm ready to go," Jill agreed reluctantly.

Allan led the way down the dark passage. "It doubles back. Why would it go . . . oh, wait. These are stairs. Careful." Joey followed the sound of his brother's footsteps up the narrow stairs. The dusty wood felt odd under his bare feet.

"The stairs end here," Allan said, "but the passage goes on."

"How far?" Joey asked.

"I can't tell."

"Do you feel any doors?" asked Jill.

"No . . . wait. This might possibly be a door." Allan paused. "I think I found a latch. Here we go."

A loud creak echoed in the darkness, and a door

swung towards them. Hardly any light entered the passage. Allan looked out. "We're inside a cupboard." He opened the cupboard door.

"What can you see?" Joey asked.

"Not much. I think we're in the old servants' quarter on the third floor, but I can't be sure. If it is, well, it's been shut up for ages."

"Let me see." Joey pushed past his sisters and looked out of the cupboard. He was disappointed. "I can't see anything."

"There probably isn't much to see anyway," Anna said. "If this *is* the old servants' quarter, it's probably just a bunch of dark, cheerless cubbyholes. And since it's been shut up so long, a number of critters have probably taken up residence there."

"Don't," Jill said.

"You wouldn't be afraid of cute little mice, would you?"

Joey closed the cupboard door. "Let's see where else this passage goes." He took off down the dark corridor.

"Be careful," Jill warned. "This passage has to either end or go back down at some point, but whatever it is, you don't want to run headlong into it."

He barely heard his sister's warning. A wall suddenly appeared in front of him, a little too close. Against his face. With a smack. "Ouch," he mumbled. He felt around the wall until he determined that the passage took a turn. He walked more slowly this time. Even so, he wasn't prepared when the floor dropped to form a stair. "I found stairs," he called back.

"Where?" Allan asked.

"There's a right, and then a left. But the left is down some stairs." Footsteps sounded behind in the passage. The floor leveled out. "I've reached the bottom," Joey called. He set his foot down, but the floor was lower than he expected. "No, wait. There's more."

"It must go all the way to the first floor," Allan said.

"I think there's a door here . . . of sorts," Joey said.

"Can you get it open?"

Slivers of light appeared, then widened as a portion of the wall rotated.

"It's a bookcase," Jill said. "A bookcase that hides the entrance to the secret passageway."

"Very original," Anna commented.

Allan, Jill, Joey, and Anna stepped through the opening left by the bookcase into Grampa's study.

"Well, that was an adventure," said Allan.

~

1920

Calvin's fingertips brushed the ivory keys of the piano. The smooth coolness was soothing. He played a chord. The notes filled the room. He ran his right hand up a scale. He paused, then launched into "Für Elise." His fingers knew where to go on their own. He took a deep breath as the music helped him relax. Everything would be okay. The mysterious writing had nothing to do with their family's history of early deaths.

A sour note marred the melody. Calvin looked down the piano. His four-year-old sister Rebekah stood with her finger on a key, grinning mischievously. He patted the piano bench, and Rebekah climbed up beside him. Calvin and Rebekah banged on the piano together. It sounded terrible, but he didn't care.

Rebekah pounded her fist on the keys, then looked up at Calvin and giggled.

"Now I'll play something for you," Calvin said. "Choose a song."

Rebekah pressed her finger to her lips as a contemplative expression passed over her face. "Play 'Amazing Grace,'" she decided.

Calvin obligingly played the melody, filling it out with a harmony of broken chords. He played through it a few times. Rebekah's childish voice joined in with the last verse.

"When we've been there ten thousand years
Bright shining as the sun,
We've no less days to sing God's praise
Than when we've first begun."

The notes faded away. Calvin sighed, his fingers resting on the keys. To have no less days even after ten thousand years was foreign to him, but a wonderful thing to think about.

~

Calvin ran his hand over the leather-bound volumes in his father's study. He wanted a new Dickens book to read. He had just finished *Great Expectations* and enjoyed it immensely. *Oliver Twist.* He liked stories about orphans. He slid the book out of its place on the shelf. He opened it and turned away.

Light flickered behind him. He froze. He didn't want to turn around, didn't want to face another hallucination, didn't want to further his fears of early death . . . yet he did.

The compulsion was too strong to resist. He turned slowly. Words etched on the face of the bookshelf, shining out at him.

Why did this have to happen to him? Why couldn't he just live a normal life? As the words faded away, he clutched the book to his chest and fled from the room.

Chapter Four

New Information

2000

Jill and Anna slipped upstairs to exchange their pajamas for church dresses. The boys headed straight to the kitchen for breakfast. Joey piled a bowl full of cereal, poured a glass of milk, and carried his breakfast over to the kitchen table where he sat next to Allan.

Gradually he became aware that his brother's gaze was focused on him.

He paused in eating. "What is it?"

"It isn't gentlemanly to eat like a ravenous pig."

Joey set his spoon down and wiped his mouth with the back of his hand. "Sorry. Adventures make me hungry."

"Everything makes you hungry," Allan said. But he grinned as he said it.

Joey had finished his cereal and put his bowl in the dishwasher before the girls joined them. He stood by the counter finishing his milk and watched as Jill filled her cereal bowl with a much more moderate amount than he had. Jill was pouring milk into her cereal when their dad came in.

"Good morning," he said.

"Good morning," Jill replied.

"Daddy, guess what Joey saw on the back of the wardrobe!" Anna exclaimed. Joey gave her a warning glance. "I mean *in* the back of the wardrobe," she corrected herself. "We found a secret passage!"

"Ah, yes," said Mr. Hubbard. "I do recall the secret passage."

"You know about it, Dad?" Allan said.

"I do, indeed. It begins in the pantry and winds through the house until it ends in the ballroom. It was used in the Underground Railroad, and further back, in the American Revolution, by the Patriots. Georgia was more friendly to Tories than Patriots in those days."

"I know that already, Dad," Joey said. He took a drink of milk.

"Georgia was the newest colony, so the people had come over more recently from England," Allan said. He went over to the sink and began to rinse off his breakfast dishes.

"I'm glad our family was made up of Patriots," Anna chimed in, returning the orange juice to the refrigerator.

"I explored that passage as a child, but my sister Bethany was more interested in it than I. She always thought there was something especially mysterious about it. Shortly before she died, she told me she had found mysterious writing on the doors into the passage. I suppose her delusion had something to do with her death, that it put her off her guard or something. I wouldn't be surprised if it was a hallucination that caused her to drown in the creek."

Allan's dishes clattered into the sink, and Joey set his glass down on the counter. Jill paused with her spoon halfway to her mouth, while Anna stood still in the middle of the floor.

"Good morning." Mrs. Hubbard's entrance into the kitchen broke the spell.

"Good morning, Mom," Allan said.

"Is Emily up yet?" Mr. Hubbard asked.

"Yes. She ought to be down here soon."

"Good. We don't want to be late for church."

"Why don't we just leave her here?" Joey said.

His parents looked at him in surprise. "Don't everybody look at me like that. It was supposed to be a joke. Besides, she'd rather stay home."

"She doesn't believe in anything she hasn't seen with her own two eyes," Anna put in.

"Eat your breakfast, Anna," Mrs. Hubbard said.

"Yes, ma'am."

Jill took her cereal bowl to the sink and turned on the water. As she rinsed her bowl and spoon, Joey set his glass next to her. He gave Jill an impish grin. A loud stomping footstep caused him to look up. Emily stood in the door to the kitchen. She was dressed in a shirt and shorts that looked as if they should have been passed down to Anna long ago. Her hair was pulled back into a loose ponytail at the nape of her neck. Her whole air reflected defiance.

"Emily Grace Hubbard, get right back upstairs and dress properly for church!" Mrs. Hubbard wasn't about to let her daughter out looking like that.

"And if I don't?"

"You will be grounded for the whole week. No TV, no telephone, no friends."

Emily turned and headed back upstairs. Jill rinsed out Joey's glass and set it in the dishwasher.

~

1800

"I should be a cabin boy sailing the open sea by now, not running errands for the house servants." George climbed the servants' stair to the third floor, his friend Matt behind him.

"Ya didn't hafta run the errand, Massa George," Matt said. "It's my mammy as needs a clean apron."

"I know. But still, it isn't as if I'll be inheriting the estate. I've got to have some career. And if I was at sea, these things wouldn't be happening."

"What things? 'Cause if it's runnin' errands fer my mammy, ya don't hafta do it. I can take care of my own mammy."

George shook his head. "It's not that . . . not really."

"Then what is it?"

"Never mind," George pushed open the door at the top of the stair and stepped into the narrow hall of the servants' quarter. He had been there often, more often than his sophisticated and proper mother liked, but George thought it a good thing to see how the servants lived. If ever he *did* become master of Creighton Hill, however unlikely, it would serve him well.

George and Matt walked down the hall, to the

room occupied by Matt's mother, the head cook.

"They're in the cupboard," Matt said. "The passage one."

George opened the cupboard and picked up a clean apron. A flash of light from the back of the cupboard caught his attention.

"I'm not crazy, am I Matt?"

"No, Massa George, you never seems crazy to me."

"Tell me, do you see light in the back of the cupboard?"

"No," Matt said. "Do you?"

"No," George lied. He stared at the cupboard. Letters formed out of the light, then faded away.

He closed the cupboard. Matt looked curiously at him.

"You all right, Massa George?"

"Yes." George followed Matt out of the room. He wasn't crazy—he didn't think—but things were getting progressively stranger.

~

2000

Emily stared moodily out the window of the Hubbards' Suburban as they sped along the road.

She had acted moody all throughout church. Yes, their church was small, and all understood the situation, but still she had made things exceedingly miserable.

Joey peeked at the book Jill was reading. *Ballet Shoes*. Ugh. Just like a girl to read and reread a book about ballet. Still, she was pleasanter to be around than Emily. At least she let people treat her like a girl. He was glad to have at least one nice sister. And, really, if he had to admit it, no one was sweeter than Jill.

Upon reaching home, the four younger children went directly to Jill and Anna's room and examined the back of the wardrobe. The mysterious writing had not reappeared.

Anna gave the perpetually, for her, blank wood a rueful look. "I wish I'd seen it. I wonder why I didn't."

"I have no idea," Joey said.

Jill perched on her bed. "Whatever the reason, it isn't there now."

Allan sat down on the floor.

"Dad said Aunt Bethany reported seeing mysterious writing shortly before she disappeared," Joey mused, pacing. "I wonder if the two events are connected."

Anna turned away from the wardrobe. "Dad

always says Aunt Bethany drowned in the creek."

Allan looked up at her. "That's just conjecture. The most logical explanation they could think of."

"Even though they dredged the creek and couldn't find her?" Joey said. "She disappeared."

"Eyes that they should not see, and ears that they should not hear," said Allan.

"Technically, they didn't see," Joey said. "They didn't see the writing on the wardrobe, and they didn't *see* them disappear."

Allan shrugged. "It's deductive reasoning. They were gone, and their bodies couldn't be found. They should have known the children disappeared, but they were blinded to it."

"Not me," said Anna. "I didn't see it, but I believe."

Joey gave her a mischievous grin. "You have eyes that see."

"Grampa believed they were disappearances," Jill said. "He was different from our other ancestors. Grampa knew our family's history. He knew the pattern, that someone disappeared every twenty years. He told us about it countless times. He believed that something other than death was taking those people."

"I think you've got something there, Jill," Allan said. "It *was* Grampa who told the stories. We wouldn't even know about it if it wasn't for him. He investigated our history. And he was so meticulous and organized that I bet there are records of everything he found."

"At this point, we need all the help we can get," Joey said.

Allan jumped to his feet. "To Grampa's study. Come on!"

Chapter Five

Next in Line

Allan searched the bookshelves in Grampa's study. He ran his hand lightly over the collection of Dickens' works, Sherlock Holmes, Jane Austen collection, and came to rest on a small leather-bound book. He carefully removed it from the shelf and opened it to the first page. The paper was yellow and brittle. Allan began to read.

"'June 28, 1800,' Holy smokes! This book is two hundred years old!"

Joey searched the shelf for more old books as Allan continued to read.

"'I feel compelled to write this for some reason unbeknownst to myself. Perhaps someone in the future will have need to see this. Something strange happened to me today. I am not mad. I know I am not mad. What I saw was there, it was truly there! In the back of the nursery wardrobe, on the panel that opens into the hidden passage, a strange message appeared. It spoke of the appearance of a land. I have mentioned it to no one. It was meant for me, I believe, but how or why I cannot tell.'"

Joey pulled what looked like another old diary off the shelf and opened it up. He flipped through a few pages. "This was written by Abigail Hubbard. Age twelve, year 1820. She talks about the shiny writing, too."

"Here's something Grampa wrote," Anna said. "It's dated October 12, 1980. 'Bethany is gone. We have dredged the creek, but she is not there. The police search for her, but they will not find her. She has disappeared at the same age as my brother Jonathan, twenty years before. There is some mystery about this house, some mystery of which my forefathers denied existence. I do not deny it. It may not be given to me to find the answer, but nevertheless, I shall try.'"

Allan opened a drawer in Grampa's file cabinet and flipped through the files. He pulled one out, set it on the desk and opened it up. Jill sat down in the desk chair beside him and looked at the file. Joey and Anna gathered around. The first document contained a list of names and dates.

1800, George Hubbard
1820, Abigail Hubbard
1840, Thomas Hubbard
1860, Mary Hubbard
1880, Theodore Hubbard
1900, Samantha Hubbard
1920, Calvin Hubbard
1940, Eleanor Hubbard
1960, Jonathan Hubbard
1980, Bethany Hubbard

"Who are all these people?" Anna asked. "And what are these dates?"

Joey began to pace the room. "Jonathan and Bethany. That wouldn't be Aunt Bethany and Great Uncle Jonathan, would it?"

"It's possible," Jill said.

"Well, I don't know of any other Bethany and Jonathan Hubbard," Joey continued.

"Grampa used to tell us about George who disappeared," Anna said.

Allan pointed at the list. "These dates are every twenty years. Wasn't that what Grampa said the length of time between disappearances was?"

"Yes." Jill nodded. "Every twenty years, a child of twelve years of age, born a Hubbard, in this very house, has disappeared mysteriously, leaving no trace.

That's what Grampa told us."

"Aunt Bethany disappeared in 1980," Joey said, "and Uncle Jonathan in 1960."

Jill picked up the document. "There are ten names on the list. Grampa said it was ten Hubbards that disappeared."

"Then I think it's a pretty safe bet that these are the names of those ten," Allan said, "and the year they disappeared."

Jill looked at the paper underneath the list. It was a family tree, specific to the members of the family related to the strange disappearances.

"Can I see that?"

Jill handed it to Joey.

The next page was full of writing, in Grampa's hand. She skimmed it quickly. "Listen to this: 'In some form or fashion, all reported the appearance of mysterious writing on the doors to the secret passage.' And we saw it," she added.

"Do you notice how periodic it is?" Joey asked. "One person disappears every twenty years. The gender alternates. And if you look at this," he laid the family tree in front of them, "you see they were all the same age, twelve years old. And had a brother, four years older. It's not a coincidence."

"Let me see that." Jill pulled the family tree over to her, and studied it. "That's so weird. Our parents and grandparents and so on got married at different ages, but they all managed to have kids exactly twenty years after the counterparts from the generation before."

"That is weird," Allan said.

"No one noticed it?" Anna said. "I think that's even weirder."

"True," said Allan. "Either our ancestors were really blind to facts, or something was keeping them from seeing."

Joey stood still suddenly in front of the desk. "It's twenty years later."

"What do you mean?" Anna asked.

"I mean it's twenty years after Aunt Bethany. She disappeared in 1980. This year is 2000."

Jill's eyes grew wide. "Oh, no."

"I think you had a good reason to be nervous about moving here, Jill," Anna said.

"Allan is twelve," Joey said, "and he saw the writing."

Jill, Joey, and Anna turned to look at Allan. All the color had drained from his face.

"But we haven't got a brother older than Allan," Anna objected. "Only a sister. And she isn't sixteen."

"No," Joey agreed. "Our family is different."

The children were silent for a moment.

"Yeah, we are," Anna said. "Maybe you won't disappear after all, Allan."

"He saw the writing," Joey said. "I bet you an

ice cream cone he does."

"You're on," said Anna.

Jill glanced through the papers on the desk. "Grampa seems to think it was only those who saw the writing that disappeared and that only those who disappeared saw the writing."

"Do you have to speak in flip flops?" Joey asked with a mischievous grin.

Jill gave him a look. "What I mean is we saw the writing. We could disappear too."

~

1940

Eleanor threw the back door open and tramped into the kitchen. The wood floor felt cool beneath her dirty bare feet. Her unruly red hair brushed her ruddy cheeks. Two boys trooped in after her. They held tin pails that sloshed water on the ground.

"We got fish, Mother." Eleanor held up her pail.

"I got more, Mother," the older of the two boys said.

"I got one more than Abe, Mother," the youngest boy said.

A woman with a careworn face turned away from the kitchen counter to look at the three children. "You all did well to catch the fish you did. Set them by the door and go clean the mud off your feet and change into dry clothes. Eleanor, I'll need your help with dinner."

"Yes, ma'am," the children chorused. They dashed out of the room.

Eleanor was back five minutes later in dry overalls, her feet clean. "What do you need me to do, Mother?"

"Could you get the cornbread out of the pantry?"

"Yes, ma'am."

Eleanor walked into the large pantry. She sighed as she gazed about the half empty shelves. It was only from stories that she knew they had once been overflowing. Once the house had been busy with servants, every meal a feast. She knew it was hard on Father. He had grown up in a better time, despite the hardships of the Great War and the early death of his brother Calvin. Growing up in the thirties, it was normal for her to depend on their fishing for food and to do all the housework themselves, but she wished for Father's sake it was not so. At least they had managed to keep the family estate.

She reached up to take the cornbread off the shelf. A bright light from the door to the secret passage caught her attention. She closed her eyes. It wasn't happening again. It had just been her imagination.

She had to look. She opened her eyes and turned to the back wall. The bright light etched words in smooth, flowing script.

"Mother? Please come here."

Eleanor's mother appeared in the doorway. "What is it?"

"There, on the door to the passage. Magic words."

"I don't see anything, honey."

"It's there," Eleanor said. "And it was there on the back of the wardrobe this morning."

"Eleanor, are you all right?"

Eleanor took a deep breath. "No."

"Come sit down."

Eleanor followed her mother out of the pantry. They sat down at the kitchen table. Eleanor folded her hands in front of her and crossed her ankles. Her mother looked at her, a concerned expression on her face.

"What was that about magic words?"

Eleanor squeezed her hands together. "This morning, when I was getting my clothes out of the wardrobe, there was a light in the back of it. It made words. It said, 'When these words are spoken, a land will appear.' Then it happened again, just now, in the pantry." Her voice was shaky. "I don't know what's happening to me. I'm afraid I'm going to die. Whatever happened to Uncle Calvin and all the others will happen to me, I'm sure of it. They all saw the magic writing. I'm so scared."

She buried her face in her hands. Her mother put her hand on Eleanor's shoulder.

"You aren't crazy, Eleanor. And you aren't going to die."

Chapter Six
A Deep State of Denial

2000

"Dad?" Anna asked at dinner that night, "why is this house still in our family? I mean, with all the strange disappearances, wouldn't our family have sold it by now?"

"Oh, please," Emily groaned. "Not more of your superstitious garbage. Get a life, one that doesn't involve conspiracy theories."

"It is a fair question," Mr. Hubbard said, "and quite a logical one. It would seem that those deaths or, as you say, disappearances, would cause our family to move. Indeed, this house has been on the market two or three times throughout its history. But it never was purchased."

"The sale was providentially hindered," Jill said.

"Other people saw the mystery our family refused to see," Joey said.

"It may seem that way," said Mrs. Hubbard. "But there is a reasonable explanation behind every so called disappearance."

"That's right," said Mr. Hubbard. "George, for instance, talked of running away to sea. It can be assumed that he did so."

"Grampa said he wasn't the sort to run away," Anna put in.

Mr. Hubbard continued as if he had not heard. "There used to be many wild animals in these parts. They could easily have carried off children. It was a serious danger in more places than here. And even today, many children are kidnapped and never seen by their families again."

"But what about the pattern?" Anna argued. "Every twenty years? Always twelve years old?"

"Many things in nature occur according to mathematical patterns," Mr. Hubbard said. "The spiral of a snail's shell, the family tree of a male bee . . . the list is endless."

"But people dying?" Joey said. "That's ridiculous."

Jill stood up. "I'll clear the table," she offered.

"I'll help." Joey had to leave the room before

he caused more problems, even if it meant helping with hated dishes. They gathered up the plates and headed to the kitchen.

"How can they be so blind?" he said as soon as they were safely within. "They have all the evidence that this is more than just natural occurrence, yet they explain it away with kidnappings and runaways."

"They have eyes, but they see not," Jill said, "ears, but they hear not."

She deposited her dishes in the sink and turned in the direction of the dining room, but a flash of light from the pantry attracted her attention. "Joey, look."

The two hurried into the pantry. On the back wall of the pantry was a point of light, lengthening and curving to form letters, just like the light in the wardrobe. This time, however, the words were different.

The wind through the trees,
Birdsong loud and clear.

The words shone out for a few moments, then faded away.

Joey and Jill stood silent for a moment. Then Jill said, "It's another line to what we saw this morning. The last words rhyme.

'When these words are spoken,
A land will appear.
The wind through the trees,
Birdsong loud and clear.'

It's a poem!"

"It might be," Joey said. "I think you'd better write it down so we don't forget. It could be important."

Jill dashed out of the kitchen and up the stairs to her room.

~

"Should we tell them?" Anna asked.

The four young Hubbards were holding a conference in the girls' room. The mysterious writing was the topic of discussion, the question: whether or not to inform their parents of it.

"I don't think so," said Allan. "Ordinarily I'd say yes, but they would only think we were making it up. Especially since we were just told Aunt Bethany said she saw the same thing. I think they'd rather we drop the subject entirely."

Joey huffed. "I know Emily would."

"What I don't understand," said Anna, "is how they can explain it all away so calmly and rationally."

Allan shook his head. "They're in a deep state of denial. They can't believe it because they won't let themselves."

"It's a terrible thing," said Jill. "None are so blind as those who will not see."

"You've got to admit, the whole thing is pretty strange," Anna said.

"Yeah," Joey agreed. "Like, where does the writing come from? And where did the others go? Why does that rhyme say 'When these words are spoken, a land will appear'? Do you think maybe there's a voice activated portal somewhere?"

Anna looked at him skeptically. "That was here in the 1800s?"

Joey shrugged.

"It's possible," Jill said. "Even if it's not voice activated, the words could still have something to do with a portal."

"But would it be a good thing?" Joey asked. "I mean, is it ever a good thing for someone to mysteriously disappear out of the world?"

"Yes," said Jill, "if they were sent to another world where they have to fight evil. It happens all the time in books."

The four children stared at each other in silence.

"Whom He calls . . ." Allan whispered.

"Whom he calls what?" Emily's voice grated from the doorway.

"Whom he calls an annoying teenager he wants to go away," Joey said.

"That's not what Allan meant," Emily insisted. "You're talking about your ridiculous conspiracy theory again, aren't you? You're stupid to believe Grampa's tall tales about people disappearing. I have the craziest siblings ever."

"We have the rudest sister ever," Anna said.

"I . . ."

"Anna," Jill said reprovingly.

"Sorry."

"Hey, you want to get stuck in a secret passage?" Joey asked. "We almost did this morning. It was so cool. We might not have ever had to see you again."

"I'm telling," Emily said.

"Fine, rat yourself out," Joey responded.

Allan sighed. "Joey and Anna, stop egging her on. You're as much to blame as Emily."

"Thank you, Allan," Emily said. "There's one person I don't have to 'rat out.'"

"You shouldn't be making fun of us any more than they should be egging you on," Jill said. "Remember what Mom said? Treat us with respect?"

"I'm sick of looking at you." Emily turned and strutted away.

"Mutual," Joey grumbled.

~

1820

Abigail picked up the clothes strewn about the nursery. She could have let Mammy do it, but she didn't mind. She rather liked taking care of her younger siblings, even if it was only picking up after them.

A little girl ran into the room. "Abby, do you know where my dolly is?"

"I think I saw it in the day nursery," Abigail said.

"I just looked in there," the little girl complained.

"Let me hang these things up in the wardrobe, and I'll help you look," Abigail promised.

"Okay."

Abigail opened the door to the wardrobe and hung up the clothes. As she turned away, a light caught her attention. She looked back.

"Adam, are you in the passage?" No answer. She looked closer at the back of the wardrobe. The passage door was closed, but there was light coming from it. "Hope, come here."

The little girl joined Abigail. "What is it, Abby?"

"Do you see the light in the wardrobe?"

"No. What does it look like?"

"It's light, and it's making words."

"Like what Uncle George wrote about?"

Abigail's heart skipped a beat. Uncle George had disappeared without a trace.

"Y . . .yes," she stammered.

"Careful, Abby," Hope said. "I don't want you to die like Uncle George."

"I'm not sure he did die," Abigail said. "A land will appear. He could be somewhere else."

"Then you can find out."

Chapter Seven
The Attic

2000

"Anna, it's time for your dentist appointment."

Anna looked over at Jill. "Try not to find anything cool while I'm gone."

"I'll try not to," Jill said. "But I don't know if I can help it."

Anna dashed out of the room. Jill picked up one of her books and put it back on the shelf. Joey poked his head into the room.

"Allan and I are going to explore the passage again. Want to come?"

Jill grimaced. "No thanks."

"You're missing out on an adventure."

"I'll pass."

"Alright."

As the boys headed to the passage, Jill wandered down to Grampa's study. She ran her hand over the delicate volumes lining the shelves. How she delighted in books! She came across one that had no title on the binding. She pulled it out and opened it to the first page. It was a diary, written by Mary Hubbard. Jill went over to the window seat and sat down.

The diary was a small, leather-bound book, with fragile, yellowed pages. Jill was almost afraid to touch it, but the content intrigued her. She felt, at first, a twinge of guilt for intruding into Mary's private things, but Mary had been long gone, and what she had written about might prove useful. The morning sun slanted in the window, illuminating the frail pages in her hands. The words were carefully formed, written with a brown, homemade ink.

"Friday, June 22, 1860.

"Today has been especially difficult. We had the sheriff here on reports of suspicious activity. He insisted on searching the house as there is a missing slave in the area, but he found none. The passages constructed to help the Patriots in the time of the War for Independence do well in these times. I was in the nursery with Harriet and James when he came. Mammy tried to keep him out, but Papa let him in. He had confidence in the sufficiency of concealment of the door, and it was not misplaced. Harriet and James were frightened, though.

"These are difficult times for children to live in. Helping slaves to escape has indeed put our family in danger, but what frightens me more is this country's departure from our founding principles. Our liberties are slipping away, just as they did in the days before the War for Independence, and our states will not sit idly by and watch it happen once more. I am terrified we shall have to fight another war to regain them.

"Saturday, June 23, 1860.

"Isaiah and Zeke left us today. I pray that they shall make it safely to Canada. It is a strange world where men can be free in Canada but they cannot in America. I fear none of us shall be free much longer. What a world this is.

"Monday, June 25, 1860.

"I encountered a strange occurrence today. I went into the secret passage to help clear signs of Isaiah and Zeke's presence from it, and on my return through the nursery, strange words appeared on the passage door. They were carved of light, but only lasted a few seconds before fading away again. I have told no one. I am afraid they should think me a lunatic. Indeed, I am inclined to think so myself. Mammy would never say such a thing, nor Harriet or James, but they should not think I was telling the truth. I should rather keep a secret than be thought a liar.

"Tuesday, June 26, 1860.

"Shall I not be free of this apparent lunacy? Two more messages appeared to me today, on the passage doors in the pantry and the servants' quarter. I am afraid to enter the ballroom or the study, for surely they shall be next. Life was normal but two days ago. I would welcome being jailed for assisting runaways, or caught in a war over independence rather than losing my mind.

"Wednesday, June 27, 1860.

"I could not avoid the study. Papa asked me to fetch a book for him, and words appeared on the door to the passage. This afternoon, a worse thing occurred. I went into the attic in search of an item stowed there last winter, and found an oaken chest. It had never been there before, I know it hadn't. I opened the chest and found weapons inside. What terrified me most was that one quiver of arrows had my name on it. I can hardly write for trembling. I almost told Mammy, but I could not. She would think me losing my mind. I contemplated taking the arrows with my name upon them, but I could not. Perhaps tomorrow my quaking will subside enough for me to take it. I feel it must be mine."

Here the diary ended. Jill looked up. She gasped.

The now familiar gleam of light had caught Jill's eye as it began to etch out upon the bookshelf that was an entrance to the passage new words.

"A stryte rules this country,
But now hope gleams."

After a moment, it faded away. Scarce seconds later, the shelf rotated and the boys came out.

"We saw something," Joey said. "Up in the servants' quarter."

"'"Though all this seems pleasant,
Things aren't as they seem,"'

Allan quoted.

"'"A stryte rules this country,
But now hope gleams,"'

Jill finished.

"What's a stryte?" Joey asked.

"Mary's diary says she found a trunk in the attic with weapons in it," Jill said. "She said one had her name on it."

Joey's eyes grew huge. "Let's go look for it!"

The three rushed out of the room and headed for the attic. They met Emily at the stairs to the third floor.

"Where are you going?" she asked.

"The attic," Jill said.

"I'm coming, too," Emily announced.

"What for?" Joey asked.

"I have nothing better to do."

The three younger children glanced at each other, then continued on their way, Emily following. Allan led the way up the spiral staircase to the attic.

There was a good deal of furniture in the attic of Creighton Hill, but the thing that stood out to the four Hubbard children was a large, beautiful, oaken chest standing against the back wall of the attic. The children went to it and Allan and Joey carefully raised the lid. On the inside of the lid, in a beautiful, flowing script, was carved a verse.

Seven girls and seven boys.
The things herein are not toys.
Choose your weapon, choose aright.
T'won't be long before the fight.

There were two rows in the chest that seemed to have at one time contained seven weapons each, but now there were only four sets left. In the back, two swords and two shields. In the front, two bows and two quivers full of arrows. The children's names were inscribed on the weapons in flowing script, the boys' names on their shields, the girls' on their quivers.

"Okay, this is weird," Emily said. "What's my name doing on a quiver?"

"Don't ask me," Joey said.

Allan took his shield from the chest, and Jill girt the sword belt about him.

"Many thanks, my lady," Allan said.

"The honor is all mine, fair brother," Jill replied.

Emily scowled. "You two are ridiculous."

"Do mine, Jill," Joey begged. "Just like lords and ladies in books."

He handed her the sword belt and she fastened it around his waist.

"Like you couldn't do that yourself," Emily said.

"Don't you ever like to pretend?" Jill asked.

"I like to pretend I'm not related to you."

Joey rolled his eyes.

"Here you go, Jill." Allan handed Jill her bow and arrows. Jill smiled at her brother. "Do you want yours, Emily?"

"I can get it myself." Emily reached forward, and took the remaining bow and quiver. At that moment, the shining letters appeared on the wall behind the chest, this time more complete than they had ever been before.

Emily took a quick step back. "Okay, now you're making me see things too. Your crazy stories are rubbing off on me."

"No, we're not," Jill said. "It's really there. I'll prove it to you." She read the words out loud.

"When these words are spoken,
A land will appear,
The wind through the trees,
Birdsong loud and clear.
Though all this seems pleasant,
Things aren't as they seem,
A stryte rules this country,
But now hope gleams.
Ten at the first and four at the last,
From foreign parts, traveling fast,
Defeat the strytes, for this is your quest,
You will not go home till you've done your best."

"It sounds like . . . instructions," Joey said.

"But very cryptic," Allan added.

"Right," said Emily.

With a blinding flash, the wall before them became a mountain forest in midmorning, a beautiful sight to behold. Behind them was the attic, just as it had been before.

"Should we go through?" Jill asked.

"Oh, so now you want to walk into a dream?"

"Why not?" Joey said. "If it is a dream, Emily, you'll just wake up and it won't have happened."

Allan and Jill exchanged a glance. "Let's do it," he said. The children took each other's hands and together stepped into the forest. The attic vanished behind them.

Chapter Eight
Captive

1800

THE FLASH OF LIGHT WAS STARTLING, EVEN more so than the appearance of the strange words. In place of the wall was a wooded mountain, unlike any he had seen. This was the strangest experience. He must be crazy.

The wood beckoned to him. He felt a strange compulsion to leave the safety of the attic and step into the dream. Leave reality. Leave sanity. Leave everything he had ever known.

He walked forward. His steps no longer fell on a wood floor, but on a grassy slope. He looked back. The attic had vanished. No turning back now.

He continued down the slope. His awareness was more acute than it had ever been. The air was fresh and clear, the birdsong was sweet and melodic, the leaves crunched under his feet. If this was a dream, it was more vivid than any he had before experienced. Though, with all the sleeping and waking between discoveries, he had a difficult time convincing himself of such.

Was he mad, then?

I am George Hubbard, age twelve years. It is the year 1800. I come from the state of Georgia in the glorious United States of America. I live on the plantation Creighton Hill. My brother is the heir to the estate. I wish to go to sea.

True, all true. Yet he was not quite convinced he was truly sane.

He emerged from the trees into an expanse of green. As far as his eyes could reach there was nothing but grass. There was not a sign of life. If this was real, he ought to investigate. He rested his hand on the hilt of the sword he had taken from the attic chest. The cool metal under his fingertips certainly felt real. He set out across the field.

For hours upon hours he walked, encountering nothing but more grass and the occasional bird or squirrel. The mountains were continually at his right, the sun to his left. He believed himself to be going north, but who could tell? Even the sun could be strange here.

He had decided to believe he was in a very real place; the ache in his muscles from walking all day convinced him of that. What sort of a place it was, he could not tell. What had the words on the wall said? *Though all this seems pleasant, things aren't as they seem. A stryte rules this country, but now hope gleams.* If it was true, he could be in danger. *Defeat the strytes, for this is your quest. You will not go home till you've done your best.* It was a scary thought. Not go home till he defeated strytes. What *was* a stryte?

A thundering of hoof beats sounded from behind. He scanned the horizon. Figures in flowing capes rode tall, dark horses in his direction. He stopped and watched them. As they drew closer, he began to notice more details. There were five figures, and all appeared to be taller than men. Their faces were pale and their hair was very dark. The most striking thing about them was their eyes. They were yellow.

George drew his sword and stood waiting for their approach. The figures surrounded him, and pointed swords at him. George raised his defensively.

"What business have you in these lands?" the leader demanded.

"It is my own, and does not concern you," George answered.

"I believe it does." The leader dismounted and

pushed back his hood. George stared up into the man's face, if it was a man. He had his doubts that it was human. His face was thin and bony, unusually pale, as if it had been painted. His hair was purely black, a stark contrast to his skin tone. Though George was tall for his age, the man towered over him. But those eyes were the worst. The eerie yellow bored into him.

The man came closer. His sword edged toward George's neck. "Mudan the Great has conquered these lands. None but strytes may go free."

These must be strytes, then. Unpleasant sorts of people.

"I am not of this land," George said. "I do not have any way to know even what land I am in."

"Likely story. You will return with us to Calhortz," the leader said.

He didn't seem to have a choice.

~

The horses galloped into town. George gritted his teeth as he held onto the stryte whose horse he was sharing. If these were in control of this world, it was no wonder the rhyme said they needed to free the people.

The town was not unlike those back home. Buildings constructed of wood lined dirt streets, signs indicating the nature of the shop hanging on poles jutting out from the buildings. Few people were about in the outskirts of town. Those who were seemed all to be hurrying in one direction. The center of town and a crowded marketplace.

The horses slowed as the group went further into town. It was plain and dusty, crowded with strytes in fancy dress and humans in poor, shabby garb. They crowded into the square. A large platform stood at one end, a stryte upon it. The strytes dismounted and forced George through the crowd to the platform. They spoke to the strytes around it in tones too low for George to hear, then several coins changed hands. George bristled. He couldn't be a slave . . . could he? He was the son of a wealthy plantation owner.

A stryte grabbed him by the shoulders and hauled him behind the platform. Manacles clapped onto his wrists. The stryte on the platform raised his hands and the buzzing of conversation ceased.

"Welcome to the slave market," the stryte said.

George looked about at the slaves surrounding him. They were all chained and miserable. None had the pale skin, extreme height, and yellow eyes of the strytes. However, there were many that still did not appear to be fully human. The man shackled next to him had longish dark blond hair, but apparently no other hair at all. His skin glistened with moisture, though the temperature was cool. He was not tall, but was nonetheless lithe and agile. George tried not to stare.

The market began. One after another, the shackled slaves were pulled up on the platform and auctioned off. Finally the man next to George was hauled up.

"What will you give me for this fine young merman?" the auctioneer bellowed. "Good for work on land or in water, he is an invaluable slave."

George held in a gasp. Merman? As in a male version of a mermaid? He hadn't thought they were real. He would believe anything at this point, even the existence of tailless merfolk.

"Two hundred omirs," someone shouted out.

"Two fifty."

"Three hundred."

The richly dressed strytes continued to shout out prices until the bidding was finally cut off. The merman was pulled into the crowd and disappeared from George's view.

George was roughly grabbed and lifted onto the platform. The stryte auctioneer squinted at him and then turned to the crowd. George looked down at himself. He *was* dressed quite differently from anyone he had seen in this world, but he didn't feel it warranted the stryte's queer look.

"I have here a strong young human lad of

remarkable potential," the auctioneer shouted. "What will you give for him?"

"One hundred fifty omirs!"

"Two hundred."

"Anyone for three hundred?" the auctioneer called out.

"Two fifty."

The strytes began even more quickly to outbid each other. George wasn't sure how the auctioneer could distinguish one bid from another. They grew louder and more frequent until the auctioneer announced, "Sold." His new owner came forward to receive him.

George looked up at his stryte master. His face bore the distinguishing features of the strytes, yet it was not as hard and cruel as his previous captors.

"My name is Royent," his new master said. "You will be treated well on my plantation, boy, as long as you do your work well. I have no quarrel with humans."

George was silent. This world was certainly a strange one.

His master was as good as his word. The slaves of his plantation, although required to work hard, were not worked harder than was good for them, and were well taken care of. He soon learned that he was in the country of Calhortz, which had lately been conquered by the strytes of the country Chalton, and its human inhabitants enslaved. Most of the conquering strytes had a strong disdain for other races, inciting them to poor treatment of their human and merfolk slaves, but George's master did not appear to share their views.

Many years passed and George began to notice a strange phenomenon. He did not get any older. He was completely unchanged from the time upon which he had entered that world, even to the length of his hair. It frightened him greatly, but he had none he felt he could confide in. Not that being unchanged was all bad; he didn't appear to be able to get hurt. Still, he wished things could be normal, that he was back in Georgia.

It was not long after George realized his unchanged age that the other slaves began to notice it as well. And they were not quick to accept his circumstance.

George lay in the bunkhouse with the other young men slaves, trying to sleep. Whispers from the other young men, however, made it difficult.

"He's not changed a bit in five years," someone whispered. "Not even his hair has grown."

"I heard the women talking about him today," another said. "Jarva said there's only one explanation. Witchery."

"Women are always coming up with rumors like that."

"What else would explain it?"

George pulled his pillow over his head and pressed it against his ears. He felt bad enough about not changing, but they were only making it worse.

It was only the beginning of his troubles. Jeers of "witch boy" constantly found him, even as he went about his own business.

Harvest time came without great incident, but without relief from the jeers. George swung a scythe at the hay they were gathering, trying to forget that he was even yet unchanged. His scythe full, he gathered a bundle and took it to the stack. A few of the young men stood about. Jeyrid was with them, the one who had insisted he was a witch. Jeyrid had never liked him, but now he had fuel.

"Why do it manually, witch boy?" he jeered. "If you can freeze your age, why not gather hay by magic?"

George tried to ignore him, but Jeyrid would not allow it. He stepped in front of him. The other boys surrounded them, cutting off escape.

"What's your secret, witch boy?" Jeyrid taunted. "Sign a pact with the devil? Or are you not human after all? You some kind of stryte or something in human form?"

"I'm not a witch boy," George said. He tried not to think about what had happened a little over one hundred years before in Salem. The accused in that incident had not been witches, but they had still been hung. They hadn't even had such obvious evidence against them. "I do not know why I haven't changed in five years, but you can be sure if I had any control over it, I would be growing normally. I did not choose this."

But had he? By going through the portal in the attic at home, had he chosen to freeze himself in time?

"Prove it." Jeyrid aimed a punch at George's jaw. George ducked. He turned and tried to leave, but the young men pushed him back. "Just try to get away from me, witch boy." He aimed another punch at George. This one came into contact with his cheek. It smarted, but did not cause the slightest bit of damage. He couldn't let Jeyrid get away with this.

George tackled Jeyrid, taking him to the ground. Before he could get in a punch, someone had hauled him off of Jeyrid.

"What is the meaning of this?" It was Royent, the master.

George looked his master in the eyes. "He hit me," he said confidently. "He was taunting me without reason and when he began physical blows I had no choice but to fight back."

"He hasn't changed a bit in the last five years," Jeyrid said. "He's a witch boy. There's no other explanation."

Royent looked down at George. "It is true," he said. There was sorrow in his eyes. "A human your age should be much changed."

George sighed. He didn't want to think about it anymore.

"You will come to the palace."

~

It was the first castle George had ever seen. It was magnificent, yet he felt no joy at the sight. He was to go on trial. And as a human slave, with such obvious evidence against him, he knew without a doubt he would be convicted. Likely executed as well.

He looked up at his master in the front of the wagon. Royent seemed harder than he ever had before. Surely *he* didn't think George was a witch boy. Strytes didn't age quickly . . . but humans did, and Royent knew it.

"Do not think I am against you, George," Royent spoke suddenly. "I like you. You have been a good and faithful slave to me all these years. I have never found cause for displeasure. But it is unnatural for a child to remain so wholly unchanged for five years. I have no choice but to turn you in."

"I'm not evil."

"I never said you were." Royent turned to look at him. "Something is wrong about you, and it is the job of the authorities to discover what it is. Perhaps it isn't even wrong, but the secret to endless life all search for. Whatever the case, it is my duty to turn you in."

"Then you don't think I'm a witch boy?"

Royent laughed dryly. "It is rare to find a stryte that believes in the supernatural. We prefer concrete things we can command and study. It is only lesser races that depend on such primitive superstitions."

George knew better than to argue. He turned his attention back to the castle.

They entered the castle courtyard. It was not empty, but it was not full of life either. Poorly dressed slaves moved slowly and purposefully about their tasks. A blond man came up to the wagon.

"I can tend to the horses, sir," he said. As George gazed at the man, he noticed something odd. His skin was damp, despite the cool breeze of autumn.

"Very well," Royent said. He climbed down from the wagon. "Come along, George."

George obeyed his master. As he passed by the man, he chanced a look up at his face. He was a merman, that was certain, but was he the same George had seen that day long ago in the slave market? The merman peered curiously at him, as if trying to remember if he had seen George before. George ducked his head and followed his master. If he was a witch boy, he didn't want any more people knowing it than necessary.

CHAPTER NINE
NAYTHIN

2000

THE GROUND SLOPED AWAY BEFORE THEM AND a canopy of leaves concealed the sky from view. The sweet song of birds filled the air. A clear, fresh mountain breeze brushed their faces. This was amazing. Despite all he had said about portals, Joey wasn't prepared for this. Not that it mattered.

"What did I tell you?" he said. "A voice activated portal in the attic that sent our ancestors to another world. Don't you wish you had believed me now?"

"I didn't disbelieve you," Allan said.

"Well, I did," Emily retorted. "And I still do. You're pulling my leg somehow. I don't know how you do it, but I want it to stop right now, or I'm telling Mom."

"Just try," Joey taunted.

Emily scowled.

Joey felt a gentle pressure on his shoulder and turned to look up into Jill's face. "It won't help anything to argue," she whispered.

Joey sighed.

"Should we explore the mountain?" Jill asked Allan.

"I don't care what you do. I'm staying right here." Emily sat down on the ground and crossed her arms across her chest.

"We won't leave you here," Allan told her.

"Why not?" Joey said. "If she wants us to, I think we should. It would serve her right."

Jill gave him a disapproving look. "Joey."

"Emily's such a spoil sport. She's a big baby and a wet blanket and . . ."

"What's that smell?" Jill interrupted.

A stench reminiscent of rotting fish seeped through the air. The birds fell silent. An ominous roar echoed through the trees and a monstrous beast appeared behind Emily. The creature had piercing red eyes and huge horns atop its massive head. Its teeth were sharp and pointed, and its arms ended in dangerous claws. It had ten legs, splayed about like a spider's, and its entire body was covered in dark hair.

Joey stood rooted to the spot. He had never really been afraid, not until now.

"Emily, stand up slowly and walk toward us," Allan directed. "Don't look back."

Emily turned her head and caught sight of the beast. An expression of terror overwhelmed her countenance. She shrieked.

The beast swiped its claw towards her. Allan dashed forward and yanked Emily out of the way.

"Run!"

Joey grabbed Jill's hand and pelted down the mountain. Allan and Emily's footsteps echoed behind them, but all were overshadowed by the thundering of the beast. Jill's palm felt sweaty in Joey's hand. It was slipping away. But he couldn't let her go. He couldn't let the beast get his sister.

Another roar boomed behind them. Joey pulled harder at Jill's hand. It seemed almost on top of them.

An arrow whizzed over their heads. A howl of pain came from the creature behind. Joey slowed their pace. Allan and Emily almost ran into them. Joey chanced a look back at the creature. Another arrow struck it and it lumbered off, back up the mountain. Something thudded to the ground.

"Ye have weapons, why do ye not use them?"

Joey turned to look at the speaker. He was

about two and a half feet tall and dressed in a tunic of an earthy green color. His face was fair and without a beard. Pointed ears poked out on either side of little green cap that sat atop his short brown curls. He held a bow in one hand and had a quiver full of arrows slung over his shoulder. He looked, Joey thought, like a miniature Robin Hood.

"I . . . I guess we do have weapons." Joey glanced sheepishly at his sword. "I forgot."

"Forgot is no excuse, laddie," the little man said. "These lasses need protection. Ye owe it to them."

Joey nodded.

"I won't forget again, sir," Allan said.

Emily peered at their rescuer. "What kind of weird midget thing are you?"

"Emily, please," Jill said. "He saved our lives. Be polite."

"Why do I need to be nice to a figment of *your* imagination?"

"I don't think this is anyone's imagination," Allan said quietly.

"Thank you, sir, for saving our lives," Jill told the little man. "But please, are you an elf?"

"Nay, lassie," he laughed. "Elves are much larger than I. I am a kalican."

"I don't believe I've ever heard of a kalican before," Jill said. "You see, we've only just arrived."

"Just arrived?" the kalican said. "From where?"

"Another world." Joey gave Emily a pointed look.

She rolled her eyes. "If you say so."

The kalican looked at them curiously for a moment, then straightened up. "Bless me, lads and lasses, I forgot to introduce me self. Me name is Naythin."

"I'm Allan. This is my brother Joey, and these are my sisters Jill and . . ."

"I'm Emily," she interrupted. "And you're just some weird dream I'm having because of my psycho siblings."

Joey glared at her.

"Ye ought to come to me village," Naythin said. "'Tis safer there than here."

"Right," Emily grumbled.

"Thank you, Mr. Naythin," Allan said. "We are very grateful for your kindness and hospitality."

Naythin started down the mountain, with the Hubbards following behind. Emily gave her siblings a dirty look.

"It's not our fault," Joey said. "You didn't have to come with us."

"I'll wake up soon, and then I'll make you pay for giving me nightmares with your ridiculous nonsense."

"I don't know about you, but this all seems pretty real to me," Joey said.

"And things aren't jumping around or morphing into weird things," Jill said. "We haven't really changed location, just what one would expect from running down a mountain."

"So maybe it's a realistic dream," Emily said.

"And if it's real?" Joey asked.

"Then I'm really making you pay."

"And how do you propose to do that?" Joey demanded.

"I haven't decided yet," Emily admitted. "But you'd better believe I can make your lives absolutely miserable."

"I can make yours miserabler," Joey said.

"That isn't even a real word."

"I don't care. It's exactly what I meant."

"Joey and Emily!" Allan reproved. "You are both in the wrong here and it has to stop. We have to be united."

"Ridiculous," Emily muttered under her breath.

"I'm sorry, Mr. Naythin," Jill said.

"That's alright, lassie. 'Tisn't yer fault."

Jill smiled faintly. "Mr. Naythin, what was that creature that was chasing us?"

"Don't ye know? Don't ye have otages where ye come from?"

"I don't believe there are any otages in Georgia. Or even in America."

"Or in our whole world, for that matter," Joey

added.

"Are they terribly dangerous?" Jill asked.

"Aye," said Naythin. "The terror of the Headstone Mountains, they are."

"If they're so terrible," Emily said, "how did you get it to go away so easily?"

"Do ye doubt me?" Naythin sounded slightly offended.

"Yes," said Emily.

"No we don't," Allan said quickly. "We were just wondering. It would be good for us to know if we ever come across another."

"Ye shoot them in the eye," the little man said. "It pains them more than anything else. Blinds them too."

Jill winced.

"Why are they called the Headstone Mountains?" Joey asked.

"Because for many, indeed, for most of the men that travel there, it is all the headstone they ever get."

"You mean like a gravestone?" Jill asked.

"Aye," said Naythin.

"Oh, please," Emily complained. "You're expecting me to believe this, too?"

"Yes," Joey said.

"It is indeed true," Naythin said. "If an otage doesn't get ye, a crefus will."

"What's a crefus?" Jill asked tentatively.

"A giant bird," Naythin answered. "They have talons sharp and strong enough to tear flesh as easily as ye would tear a sheet of paper."

Jill shuddered. Allan put his arm around his sister's shoulders.

"I can't believe this," Emily said.

"You're welcome to go back up the mountain and look for a portal that isn't there anymore," Joey said. "Be my guest."

Emily scowled.

"We are almost to my village," Naythin said.

Chapter Ten
The Tower

1805

King Mudan sat on his throne, rich royal robes draped about him. His yellow eyes stared piercingly out of his pale face. A heavy gold crown contrasted sharply with his smooth black hair.

George shrank under his gaze. He had never been in the presence of royalty, never had any desire to. He was an American. He believed in republics, not monarchies. A monarchy was dangerous. He was doomed. There was no way he could get true justice; no way he could go free.

Royent's hand on his shoulder was the only thing that kept him from bolting.

"This is the boy, my liege," Royent said. "He has been unchanged since I bought him five years ago."

Mudan surveyed him. George shifted uncomfortably, but continued to look steadily at the king.

"Lower your eyes, boy," Mudan commanded. "It becomes not a human slave to gaze so at royalty."

George dropped his eyes. He was sure President Adams wouldn't forbid a slave to look at him.

"You say he hasn't changed," Mudan continued.

"You can trust me to speak the truth, my liege," Royent said.

"He will be taken to the Tower, where he can be studied," the king decided. "You will be justly compensated for your loss."

"Yes, my liege."

"You may go." Royent squeezed George's shoulder as if to give him comfort, then left the room.

"Aldan, conduct this young slave to the Tower."

A guard came forward and silently directed George to his new home.

Aldan wove through the halls and various ornate rooms, only occasionally glancing back to be sure George was still behind him. They went on and on until George was overwhelmed with the size of the place. Creighton Hill was big, but it seemed miniscule in comparison. They ascended many flights of steps. George had lost track of the number of floors he had been on.

Finally, Aldan paused before a door and swung it open. George stood in the open doorway. A dark, wooden spiral staircase rose in front of him. He gulped. He had never liked enclosed spaces like this, and it now only served to remind him of the stairs to the attic . . . the stairs to the portal which had thrown him into this world and trapped him in time.

"Go up," Aldan told him. "There is only one way, and one door."

George stepped inside. The door slammed behind him. As he turned back, he heard the lock click. Nothing for it but to go up. He set his foot on the first step. Then the next. And the next. On and on he climbed, never ceasing, anxious only to get to the top. He came upon the door at the top so suddenly in the dark, he nearly ran into it. He felt for the handle. His fingers closed around a brass knob. He twisted it and the door swung away from him. He entered and closed the door behind him.

The room into which he had stepped was round and spacious. The walls were entirely lined with books. Various contraptions he couldn't identify stood about on tables. A man sat at a table near the center of the room, poring over a large, leather-bound book, making notes on a piece of parchment.

George approached slowly. The man looked up. He was fair, and his eyes were a clear blue. The points of his ears poked out through his blond hair. He laid down his quill pen.

"You are the boy?"

"Yes," George said.

"Welcome to the Tower," he said. "My name is Camthalion. I am an elven scholar."

George crept closer. The elf seemed kind, yet something about him commanded an enormous amount of respect. "Are you going to do tests on me?"

"Yes," Camthalion replied. George must have appeared startled, for he continued, "Do not be afraid. I shall observe your behavior, and compare it with what is generally known of the ordinary. I will not dissect you or do chemical tests."

"What about magic tests?"

"Magic, as in tampering with the physical by forbidden use of the supernatural? No, we have no tests for determining that."

"What about the water test? Only the guilty ones float."

"Float? Surely an intelligent lad such as yourself knows that to float only means one knows how to swim."

He did. "There is something wrong with me. The other slaves on the plantation called me 'witch boy.' There's something unnatural about me. I don't know what other than magic could keep me the same for five years."

"Have a seat," Camthalion said. George sat in an extra chair next to the elf. "Do you believe in God?"

"Yes."

"Do you believe He can do all things?"

"With God all things are possible," George quoted.

"Do you believe He always has a reason for things?"

George was silent for a moment. "My mother always said He does. But why would He prevent my going to sea only to have me end up stuck here, never changing?"

"God has a reason," Camthalion said. "He has a purpose for you, and He has ways of accomplishing it, even if they seem strange to us."

George sighed. "Do you think it is His will that I be stuck as a twelve year old?"

"There is no other option."

~

Life quickly settled into a routine in the tower. Camthalion woke up early for a morning devotional, breakfast came at seven, and the morning was spent in study. After luncheon, Camthalion made reports of his recent discoveries in research, then spent the rest of the afternoon furthering such. The evenings he entirely devoted to George.

Camthalion was wise and scholarly, yet he divulged little information about his personal self. George was not one to pry, but he couldn't help wondering what the elf's story was. He seemed to be the only elf in all of Calhortz.

One evening, George inquired into Camthalion's past.

"It is not one pleasant to share," Camthalion said. "It would be wrong to burden you."

"You have been bearing my burdens," George said. "It is only right for me to do the same for you."

Camthalion looked at him, his eyes for once a window into the soul he usually so carefully concealed. "I am from the forest of Olithea. It was once heavily peopled with elves. We were great artists; we believe the useful should always be also a work of art. We learned much, that we might better know the Creator by studying the Creation. We were capable fighters when cause arose, but cause did not often arise. We were at enmity with none, save the strytes. The strytes caused themselves to be at enmity with all by their disdain for all others. They considered others, humans and merfolk particularly, to be fit only for hard manual labor, not suited to govern themselves.

"The men of Calhortz were largely farmers. They cultivated the land and cultivated it well. It was a fruitful land, unlike Chalton, that of the strytes, which yields naught but coal. The strytes saw here nothing but an opportunity they missed by allowing the men to go free and they determined to let it be so no longer. They had previously enslaved merfolk in the coal mines, and did not fail to exploit their abilities in attacking Calhortz.

"Olithea lies between the two lands, so had it not been the nature of the elves to help those in need, still it would have been in our best interest to assist. Alas, the strytes were well prepared for any and all resistance against them. Our efforts were futile. Calhortz was overtaken. As a race, the elves were nearly wiped out. Few survived. I, as one of the most advanced scholars of my people, was deemed too valuable to terminate, and so I have been shut up in this tower. My family, what is left of it, is kept here as leverage. If I do all I am told, they will be safe and I can see them occasionally. If I do not, they will face execution before me."

George took a deep breath. "I will do all in my power to deliver them to freedom."

CHAPTER ELEVEN

KARRICA VILLAGE

2000

THE GRASS BENEATH THEIR FEET SOFTENED AS they approached the foot of the mountain. Emily's complaints had fortunately subsided, allowing the children to take in the beauty of the mountainside. Joey's temper had cooled substantially with Emily's silence.

"Here we are."

They stepped out of the trees into Karrica Village. The village was made up of about four dozen wigwams that seemed to be made of leafy branches woven together. A group of kalican children chased each other around the village tossing a ball to and fro, apparently engaged in some kind of game. There were cook fires scattered about the village, kalican women busy at each. A delightful aroma wafted toward the children.

"Food!" Joey exclaimed.

"Are ye hungry?" Naythin asked.

"He's always hungry," Emily said. "You can't believe anything he says about food."

"You can't believe anything Emily says about anything," Joey said. His good temper was gone again.

"I . . ."

"Stop it, you two," Allan interrupted.

Naythin gave them a curious glance.

"I am hungry," Joey persisted.

"Ye can eat with me family," Naythin offered.

"That's all right," Jill said. "We had our lunch not long ago."

"It was three hours ago," Joey said with a mournful expression on his face.

"I do not mind," Naythin insisted. "I should like for ye to meet me family."

Jill and Allan exchanged a glance, Joey pleading with the most mournful expression he could muster, Emily pouting sullenly.

"If you really don't mind," Allan relented.

"Yippee!" Joey yelled.

"Don't get so excited about it," Emily said. "It'll

just be imaginary food, just like this is an imaginary place."

Joey opened his mouth to respond, but Allan grabbed his arm and propelled him forward, whispering to him as he did so: "Don't say anything. You'll be the strong one if you restrain yourself."

Joey sighed. He knew Allan was right. Why did he always have to be right about things like this? Why wouldn't Allan just lose his temper and let Emily have it? She deserved it.

Naythin led the Hubbards through the village to one of the cook fires. A kalican woman and girl were busy about it. "Leela, dear!"

The woman turned around. "Naythin!" She sobered suddenly. "Ye dinna get any game."

"Nay, wife," Naythin said. "But I found these human children in the Headstone Mountains. They'll be staying to dinner."

"We don't mean to impose," Jill said hurriedly. Emily rolled her eyes.

"'Tisn't imposing." Leela's countenance was thoughtful as she looked up into their faces. "Meelya," to the girl, "run and fetch yer brothers and sisters."

"Aye, Mam." Meelya took off running in the direction of the playing children.

Joey's stomach rumbled. He sniffed the mouth-watering aroma drifting from the cook pot over the fire. "What's for dinner?"

Leela smiled at him. "Rabbit stew."

"Rabbit. Gross," Emily said. Even Jill didn't look pleased.

"Sounds good to me," Joey said.

"I'm happy ye think so." Leela began filling small bowls with the stew. "What were ye doing in the Headstone Mountains today?"

"We came from another world," Jill said.

"Yeah," Joey interrupted. "A portal opened up in our attic when Jill read a poem, and we came through onto the mountain."

"Right," said Emily.

"A portal from another world?" Naythin asked.

"I think it's just a dream," Emily said.

"So you just *think* it's a dream now," Joey said.

"This is not a dream," Naythin said. "And it has happened before. Twenty years ago, a girl came to our village from another world. Her name was Bethany."

The children—even Emily—stared at him with open mouths.

"You know Aunt Bethany?" Allan asked.

"This is impossible," Emily said.

At that moment, Meelya came back with five more kalican children. The oldest, a boy, turned to Naythin. "Hello, Da," he said.

"Hello, Peetur," Naythin said. "We have guests

for dinner."

Peetur turned to the Hubbards. "Hello."

"Hello," the younger Hubbards said in unison.

"Children," said Leela, "don't dilly-dally. Get yer food."

The kalican children took bowls of steaming stew and sat down on the ground. The Hubbards followed their example. Naythin folded his hands together and bowed his head.

"We thank Ye, Lord," he prayed, "for all Ye have provided for us. Thank Ye for this day, thank Ye for our guests, thank Ye for the food Ye have given us."

"Amen," chorused the kalican children.

Joey lifted a spoonful of stew to his lips. "This is delicious!" he exclaimed.

"It's food," Jill smiled.

"I'm glad ye like it," Leela said.

"Whatever happened to Bethany?" Jill asked.

"She is one of the Time Captives of Crannig Castle," Naythin said solemnly. "And ye are as well, like as not."

"What are Time Captives?" Allan asked.

"And what's Crannig Castle?" Joey asked.

Naythin set down his empty bowl. "Two hundred years ago, the strytes came from their homeland of Chalton, and conquered Calhortz, enslaving the human inhabitants and decimating the elves and kalicans who went to their aid. Not long after, a boy appeared out of nowhere. The strytes kidnapped him and enslaved him, but it was not long before it was noticed he did not change. He was a captive of time."

"You mean he was exactly the same as when he came here no matter how much time went by?" Joey asked.

"Aye," Naythin answered.

"Hogwash," Emily said.

"'Tisn't hogwash," Peetur said. "He was the first Time Captive of Crannig Castle, wasn't he Da?"

"Aye," said Naythin. "He was taken to Crannig Castle, the palace of Calhortz and imprisoned there. Every twenty years a child appears and becomes one of the Time Captives."

Joey's mouth dropped open. He looked at Jill. "Every twenty years? Isn't that what Grampa said about the people who disappeared?"

Jill nodded.

"Are we Time Captives?" Joey asked.

"I wouldn't be surprised," Allan said.

"Baloney," Emily said. "No one can get stuck in time."

"Jill, wasn't there a book about that?" Joey said. Jill would know, though Emily still wouldn't accept it, even if there was.

"It's a ridiculous concept," Emily interjected.

"There is," Jill answered, "a family drank some water that froze them in time for all eternity. The world kept going on around them, but they never changed."

Joey shot Emily a triumphant glance.

"That doesn't mean it can really happen," Emily said.

"This morning you wouldn't have believed in other worlds," Joey persisted.

"I still don't."

"Stories are often true," Peetur said. "There are Time Captives at Crannig Castle."

"I'll believe it when I see it."

"Ye will see it," Leela said. "Ye have all the indication of Time Captives, and they always meet up somehow."

"Right."

"I've got another question," Joey said. "What are strytes?"

"Ye don't want to know," Meelya said solemnly.

"Oh, come on," Joey said. "I've already seen an otage. How bad can they be?"

"They are rational beings," Naythin said. "That makes them much worse."

"Meelya, Graiss, gather the dishes," Leela said.

"I'll help," Jill offered. She and the two oldest kalican girls began cleaning up. Why Jill was always eager to help Joey would never know. Girls! So different from him . . . and from each other.

"Strytes are tall and thin and pale and have yellow eyes," Peetur offered. "They live the longest of anyone in Calhortea, even longer than the elves. The ones who took Calhortz two hundred years ago are still in power there. They use slaves instead of working for themselves, and they like fights."

"Sounds like Emily," Joey said. Emily shot him a dirty look.

"Joey," Allan reproved.

"They have no qualms about killing other races," Naythin said. "They even enjoy it as sport. They are very dangerous."

"Let's go face them!" Joey cried. But even as he said it, his heart quailed. People who killed others for sport didn't really seem very friendly. Jill gave him a look that clearly said, *Are you crazy?* Everyone else looked at him in surprise. Joey grinned sheepishly. "Or let's not. What else can we do?"

There was silence. Then Peetur spoke up.

"Auld Sauliman says that King Harald and Queen Elysia were exiled to an island at the mouth of the River Everlong. Ye could search for them or their descendants. Perhaps they will be able to take their land back."

"That's a stupid idea," Emily said.

"Why's that?" Joey asked. "I think it's a good idea."

"If they were there and could take their land back, why haven't they?"

"You actually have a good point, Emily," Allan admitted. He sounded surprised.

"Aye," Naythin agreed. "If they are there, they canna get out."

"Then we look for the Time Captives," Joey said.

Everyone looked at him strangely again.

"What? We wouldn't be here if we weren't supposed to do something. Remember what the rhyme on the wall said?"

"'Defeat the strytes, for this is your quest. You will not go home till you've done your best,'" Jill murmured.

"Exactly," Joey said.

Allan stood up. "Then we should search for our ancestors. We must do this together. And we can't do it together unless we find them."

At last, they had a mission that was agreed to be the first plan of action. Defeating the strytes was kind of impossible without the people they were supposed to defeat them with. He was ready to find them, no matter what the cost. Well, maybe not that exactly, but he was ready to find them, anyway.

"Alright. Let's go," Joey said.

"Now?" Jill said.

Allan squinted at the sky. "It's too late to start

today."

"Tomorrow, then?" Joey asked.

Allan looked questioningly at Naythin. "Aye. Ye may leave tomorrow. Indeed, I canna stop ye if ye wanted to go now."

"Uh, how do we get there?" Joey asked.

"I can go with ye," Peetur offered. "If I may." He looked toward his parents. "Da? Mam?"

Naythin and Leela exchanged a long glance. In Leela's eyes was deep concern for her son, but also calm acceptance, as if she knew this was what he was meant to do and could not dispute it. "Aye," Naythin said. "Ye are responsible, and it is time ye put off childhood. Perhaps this will satisfy yer sense of adventure."

"Thank ye, Da."

"Tomorrow morning, then," Allan said.

"First ye need training in yer weapons," Naythin said.

Allan laughed. "We do need that."

~

Naythin led the children a little ways away from the village where an archery shooting range was set up. The targets didn't really look like one would expect, they weren't bull's-eyes, but they were painted animal skins stretched across wooden frames.

Naythin instructed the girls first. Joey itched to learn archery himself, but his Time Captive weapon was a sword. He watched as Jill drew back an arrow and let it fly towards the target. It hit in the exact center.

"Bravo, Jill!" he cheered for his sister. She smiled shyly.

"Great shot," Allan praised.

"Excellent, lassie," Naythin said. "Try it again."

Jill shot another arrow. This one split the previous arrow down the center. Joey's jaw dropped. She looked startled. "How did that happen?"

"It's a dream, anything can happen," Emily snorted. As if to prove her point, she sent an arrow through the center of Jill's.

"Have either of ye done archery before?" Naythin asked.

Jill shook her head. "Never."

"I told you it was a dream," Emily persisted.

"I can fly in my dreams," Joey said. "Do you see me floating in the air?"

Emily stuck out her tongue at him.

"Are the girls enchanted?" Joey asked.

"Nay," Naythin assured him. "There are no enchantments. Yet ye may have been given gifts."

"Gifts?" Allan asked.

"Aye," said Naythin. "Ye have been called out of your own world into this. It is unlikely the

Creator would not have given ye some sort of gifts to assist in your quest."

"So the girls being good at archery is a gift?" Joey asked. "What about me? Can I try?" Naythin nodded, and Joey snatched up a spare bow. He nocked an arrow . . . and it wobbled to a stop a few feet in front of him. "That didn't work."

Jill looked thoughtfully at her bow. "Try mine."

Joey took it and sent an arrow into the girls' arrows. "Whoa."

"That gives a whole new meaning to 'it does not easily miss,'" Jill said.

"If the girls' bows work like that, how about our swords?" Allan asked.

"We'll be super skilled swordsmen," Joey said. He handed Jill her bow back and drew his sword. "En garde!"

Allan looked apprehensive, but he too drew his sword. The two boys sparred for a few moments, each fighting as if it was the most natural thing in the world. Allan stepped back and sheathed his sword.

"These weapons are more than we had guessed," he said.

Naythin smiled up at the Hubbards. "I do believe they will serve ye well."

Chapter Twelve
A New Home

1820

An oaken chest stood against the far wall of the attic. Abigail was sure it hadn't been there before. She hesitantly opened the lid. Rows of weapons lined the chest. A line of seven sets of bows and arrows sat behind a row of six swords and shields. However, there appeared to be an empty space in the row of swords . . . a space marked "George."

Now that she noticed that, she could see every weapon was labeled with a name—Thomas, Mary, Theodore, and on—including her own name. She picked up the archery set that bore her name.

A flash of light appeared above the chest: the same words that had been appearing all over the house, only it was now finished off. She murmured the words quietly as she read them. All of a sudden, there was a blinding flash and the attic wall was gone.

A land will appear. It was true, then. A land had appeared in the attic as the magic words had said. Just as it must have for Uncle George.

Abigail gripped her bow, and the leather strap with which she had slung her quiver over her shoulder. She inched forward, her shoes tapping against the floor, her heart pounding. She wasn't sure she really wanted to go, yet she felt an irresistible draw to it. Her feet were still on the wood floor of the attic, but a mountain wind whipped her blonde braids about. Her skirt pressed hard against her legs. She gripped her bow tighter and stepped forward.

The wind lessened instantly. Abigail looked around in wonder. The trees rose high above her head. Birds flitted to and fro, singing sweet melodies. She glanced back. Her heartbeat quickened as she saw the attic vanish behind her. No turning back now. She set her face forward.

Abigail began her descent from the mountain. Aside from the birdsong, the mountain was silent. Too silent. *The wind through the trees, birdsong loud and clear.* This was how it was supposed to be. She continued down the hill.

The terrain was hard and rough. She had difficulty retaining her balance. She had to sling her bow over her shoulder to free her hands so that if she stumbled she should be able to catch herself. It was not the best way to keep a bow, she knew—archery was a hobby of her brother Noah's and he had taught her bows were best kept unstrung—but she knew not against what she may have to defend herself at a moment's notice. Anyhow, she wasn't sure she remembered how to string and unstring a bow.

She brushed a loose strand of blonde hair away from her temple. The now gentle breeze was doing nothing to cool her. A mountain trek, even downhill, was more grueling than her usual activity. Her hem had become ragged and dirty. For once, Abigail did not mind that her dress was not pristine and unsoiled. She only wanted to reach civilization. She did not want to be alone.

Gradually, the slope leveled out and the ground softened. Abigail's shoes sank slightly in the soft earth with every step. It felt good to her tired feet. She was sorely tempted to remove her shoes and walk barefooted, but her dignity and fine upbringing forbade it. She was a lady, even if she was traversing a strange land alone.

The trees thinned ahead. She crept forward, not wanting to dash out into the open without first determining the propriety of such an action. She peeked around the trunk of a tree and drew her breath in sharply at the sight.

It was an Indian village . . . or was it? On closer inspection, she noted that the wigwams were not only too small for an ordinary human to inhabit; they were made of leafy branches instead of animal skins. There was no one to be seen.

Abigail crept out of the trees. She strained her ears for a sound, any sign she was not alone. She moved carefully through the scattered wigwams, glancing furtively here and there. Still she saw no one. Did she really want to see someone? Perhaps it was better to be alone. If she was alone she was not with an enemy. Yet she was lonely. Lonely enough to risk it.

"Hello? Is there anyone here?" She peeked around a wigwam. Still no one.

"Aye, there is." Abigail whipped around, then scolded herself for her unladylike behavior. That was before she got a good look at the speaker. He was only about two feet tall, and had dark curly hair and pointed ears. She jumped back.

"I dinna mean to frighten ye," he said. "Ye are human and so no enemy to me. Only strytes are me enemy."

Abigail started and her eyes grew wide. Had he just mentioned strytes? She quickly resumed her dignity. "Would you mind telling me where I am? I seem to be lost."

"Ye are in the land of Kalica, lassie. 'Tis a sorry thing that it has only just become such once more."

"How do you mean?"

"Do ye not know? Where have ye been all this time that your ignorance of current events is so plain?"

Abigail took a deep breath. She hated being thought dull and stupid. She was not. "I have been in Georgia, in the United States of America. It is my home."

It was the little man's turn to look confused. "I have never heard of such a place. Is it in Calhortea at all?"

"I do not believe so," Abigail responded. "I was in my attic at home and the wall became a mountain. When I stepped out, my home disappeared."

"Then you are another."

"Another what? And who are you?" A pang of regret for her harsh tone stabbed Abigail's heart. "I'm terribly sorry for behaving so. I have been subjected to very strange circumstances of late, and I am not myself. Forgive me."

"Ye are forgiven," the little man said. "If ye are a Time Captive from out of this world, as George before ye, ye have reason to be out of sorts."

Abigail opened her mouth to speak, but the

little man continued. "I am Luuke, one of the few kalicans to survive the Great War which devastated all who opposed the strytes. Our village is humble and scarcely populated, but ye are welcome to what we have."

"What of George? Where is he? What happened to him?"

"It is not a thing well spoken of in the open, lassie," Luuke said.

Abigail sighed. She felt so close to discovering what had become of her uncle, yet so far away. "My name is Abigail. I believe the George you speak of is my uncle. I would very much like to know what has become of him."

Luuke pressed a finger warningly to his lips. "These are difficult times," he whispered. "One never knows when spies may be about." He raised his voice to normal tones. "Come to my wigwam for a bite to eat. I am sure ye could use some nourishment."

He walked past her and wove his way through the empty village. Abigail hesitated, but she followed, holding tight to her bow. He seemed harmless, but one never knew, especially in a situation such as this.

Luuke stopped in front of one of the wigwams and pushed aside the leaves hanging in the doorway. He motioned for her to go in. Abigail ducked her head and entered the wigwam.

Though the wigwam was evidently spacious enough for a kalican, Abigail had to hunch over to fit. The sun shone through the leaves, tinting the light slightly green. The floor was carpeted with soft grass, save for a cleared space in the middle, likely for a fire, though none was presently burning. Strips of dried meat hung from the ceiling. Two woven reed mats were spread around the perimeter. A kalican girl lay on one.

"Evalin?"

The girl turned over and looked toward the entrance. Her face was flushed and her eyes unusually bright.

"Are ye any better, sister?"

"Nay," Evalin said weakly.

"I can go," Abigail said. "I do not want to bother you."

"Nay," Luuke said. "Ye should not be safe."

"Why should I not be safe?" Abigail said.

Evalin looked inquiringly at her brother. Luuke let the leaves fall back over the entrance. He moved silently around the wigwam and knelt next to Evalin. He gently laid his hand over her forehead. She closed her eyes contentedly, as if his touch was soothing to her fevered brow.

"Ye may sit," Luuke invited Abigail. "We may not have much, but the grass is clean."

Abigail carefully descended to the ground. It

had been long since she had been allowed to do so. It was not considered proper for the daughter of a wealthy plantation owner. Yet, she found it actually quite nice.

Luuke then told her the history of that land, how twenty-one years before, strytes had come and conquered the land of Calhortz enslaving its people and decimating the races of kalicans and elves that had defended them. After the Great War, a boy had appeared from another world, been enslaved by the strytes, and soon discovered to be unchanging. He was captive at Crannig Castle—a Time Captive. It appeared Abigail was likely one as well.

"And Mudan would do anything to get his hands on another Time Captive," Luuke continued. "He wishes to discover the secret behind frozen aging. More Time Captives would increase his chances."

"What shall I do then?" Abigail asked.

"Ye can stay here. I'll do me best to protect ye."

Abigail tried not to laugh at the thought of such a small person protecting her from anything. She instantly sobered as her glance fell on Evalin.

"What of your sister? I could not inconvenience you in such dire circumstances. However, if there is anything I can do to help, I would do it gladly. I have helped with the ill and injured in time past."

Luuke brushed his fingertips against Evalin's

feverish forehead. "We would be glad of yer help."

Abigail smiled sympathetically. "I will do my very best."

Chapter Thirteen
The Marsh

2000

JOEY STRETCHED AND SAT UP. HIS CLOTHES FELT damp. He blinked at the charred remains of the fire. It had blazed brightly the night before, but was now blackened and covered in dew. Allan lay near him, Naythin and his older sons across the fire pit. They had elected to sleep out of doors so that the girls could take shelter in the wigwam.

"Are ye awake?"

Joey turned his attention to Naythin. The little man had sprung up from his resting place and busied himself fetching wood from the woodpile to rebuild the fire all in a moment.

"Yes," Joey said. "I'm all wet, though. I've never slept out in the dew before. Mom would be horrified."

Naythin chuckled. "That is what happens with sleeping out of doors."

Peetur awoke next and wished them good morning. Joey and Allan echoed him.

"Are ye ready to go on an adventure?" Peetur asked excitedly.

"I am," one of the younger kalicans said.

"Nay, Atkinson," Naythin said. "Ye are too young."

"Am I too young, Da?" the youngest boy said.

"Aye, Mykall."

Mykall turned to Joey. "How old are ye?" he asked.

"Ten."

"See, Da," Mykall said. "I'm almost as old as he is, and he's going."

"Ye aren't a Time Captive."

"Sure he is," Joey said with a grin. "He doesn't look any different than he did yesterday."

Naythin shook his head. "It is not a thing to joke about."

"I thought it was funny," Atkinson defended him.

"Me too," Mykall said.

Joey grinned mischievously.

Meelya peeked out of the wigwam. "Good morning."

A chorus of "Good mornings" greeted her.

"Is Jill up yet?" Allan asked.

"Aye, but not willingly."

"Big surprise," Joey said.

A muffled scream emerged from the wigwam followed by Emily's voice. "Ugh. What are these tiny people doing? Where am I? I want to wake up for real!" This last was nearly a shriek.

Joey and Allan exchanged a glance. "Emily's up," Joey commented. Scarce seconds later, Leela and her two youngest daughters emerged from the wigwam. The littlest girl, Sofeeya, ran up to Joey.

"I don't like your sister," she whispered.

Joey's face broke out into a wide grin. "I don't like her either."

Jill ducked out of the wigwam, her eyes wide. "This is not going to be pleasant." She nodded towards Emily.

"Duh," Joey said. Sometimes it seemed like Jill turned a blind eye toward Emily. He never could, nor had he wanted to. He was glad she wasn't now.

Jill put on a bright smile, though Joey could tell it was mostly fake. "Is there anything I can do to help with breakfast?"

"Nay, lass," Leela said. "Graiss will help with the breakfast. Ye and Meelya must finish preparing the packs for the journey."

"I'll help," Allan volunteered.

"Me too," Joey said reluctantly. At least it would give him something to do while waiting for breakfast.

The Hubbards and several kalicans finished preparing five packs of food and blankets, then sat down to eat the cornmeal mush Leela and Graiss had made. Emily had not come out.

"Emily, are you going to eat before we go?" Allan called into the wigwam.

"No. I'm not going anywhere. I'm not coming out looking like this. My clothes are dirty and my hair is messy, and I haven't got any make-up."

"Mom doesn't let you wear make-up," Joey said. "And anyway, no amount of anything would hide your ugliness."

"Joey!" Jill stared at him in shock.

"Why, you . . ." Emily barged out of the wigwam, her face red with anger. She glared at Joey.

"See, I know how to get her to come out."

Jill tried to give Joey a disapproving look as she offered Emily her bowl of cornmeal mush, but did not quite succeed. Despite her show of politeness and hospitality, on the inside, she felt much the same as Joey.

"This is nasty," Emily complained as she took a bite of breakfast. Nevertheless, she ate it all.

"Are ye sure ye want to go, Peetur?" Leela

asked her oldest son.

"Aye, Mam. They need guidance, as they are new to this world and Da canna be spared."

Leela blinked back tears as she embraced her son. "Be safe." She pulled back and looked into his face. "The Lord be with ye."

Peetur nodded. Emily rolled her eyes. Joey glared at her.

"Just let it go," Jill whispered fiercely to him. She grabbed his hand and held it tight. Joey tried to squirm out of her grasp. He didn't want to be seen holding his sister's hand, but she held too tightly. Maybe it was for the best. With Jill squeezing his hand, he was too preoccupied to start a fight with Emily. Though if she started one first . . .

The rest of Peetur's family gathered to say their farewells. Joey felt a twinge of guilt. He hadn't had an opportunity to say goodbye to his family. *Just remember the ice cream,* he told himself. *If you get back, Anna owes you an ice cream cone.*

The four Hubbards and Peetur picked up their packs and stood together ready to set out on their journey. Emily pouted, Jill looked scared, and Allan looked apprehensive.

"Off ye go." Leela gave a weak smile. "Come back when ye have restored our freedom."

"I will, Mam," Peetur said.

"The Lord be with ye all," Naythin told them.

Joey slung his pack over his shoulder and followed Peetur and his family out of the village. The adventure was beginning.

~

"There is no way I'm going in there."

Ahead of them, as far as their eyes could reach, the land was covered in rushes. Small puddles of water peeked out from the edge, and gathered in pools throughout. The ground beneath their feet was spongy. The buzz of mosquitoes filled the air, coupled by the throaty call of bullfrogs. It was a marsh full of life, and Emily was completely averse to entering. True, it was less appealing than the meadow they had been travelling across the last couple of days, but it was just as necessary.

"'Twould take too long to go around," Peetur said.

Emily folded her arms across her chest. "There is no way I'm going into a marsh. And Jill, don't you tell me you're willing to go. I know you too well to think you'd be interested in tramping around on soggy ground surrounded by goodness knows what kind of bugs and animals."

Jill's countenance reflected the truth of Emily's claim. She wouldn't like going into a marsh. However, she would be easier to get to go in than Emily would be.

"Is there a Gulper in this marsh?" Jill asked.

Emily frowned. "A what?"

"A sinkhole. Like quicksand, but mud. I don't want to drown in mud." Her voice quavered with worry.

"Where did you get that idea from?"

"*Gone-Away Lake*. A little boy almost died in the Gulper."

"That was a stupid book," Emily said.

"You think any book we like is stupid," Joey said. "Peetur, there's no Gulper, is there?"

Peetur shook his head. "Nay."

"Then come on." Joey motioned to his siblings.

Emily just stood stubbornly. "I'm not going. I'm not going to ruin my sneakers tramping about in puddles, and I'm not getting my feet all wet and wrinkled, and you can just forget making me."

"There's mosquitoes," Jill said. "And frogs, and probably snakes."

"I know, Jillie," Allan said. "But you can bear with them. You are a brave girl and I'll be there with you every step of the way."

"I got seventy-five mosquito bites last time we went camping," Jill said.

Emily screwed up her face. "Great, now you remind me of that miserable trip. Forget it, I'm going home."

"Uh, we can't," Joey pointed out. "'You will not go home till you've done your best.'"

"Who cares about that old rhyme anyhow?"

"It kind of sent us here."

"Jillie, you will be a good sport about the marsh, won't you?" Allan asked.

Jill looked as if she was about to cry. "I'll try."

"Emily?"

"I already said forget it."

Joey took off his socks and shoes and hung them around his neck. "I'm ready. I won't even get my socks wet."

"Well, then, good for you," Emily said sarcastically. "But I'll stay behind if I have to."

Peetur whipped around suddenly. He scanned the air. "Get into the marsh!"

Joey followed Peetur's line of sight. An enormous bird headed towards them. It had a wingspan of six feet and sharp, cruel talons. Its hooked beak only added to its dark sinister look.

Jill's eyes widened in horror. "What is that?"

"A crefus," Peetur said. "Hide quickly among the rushes."

Joey darted into the marsh, pausing only briefly to grab Jill by the arm and drag her along. Mud squished between his toes. He crouched down in the reeds, ducking out of view. Emily stood staring up at the crefus. Allan darted toward her, and grabbed her around the waist, intending to carry her to safety. He was barely as tall as she and, though strong, not strong enough.

Emily struggled against Allan. He tried to drag her towards the marsh, but she pulled away. The crefus turned its head toward them. It gave an earsplitting shriek.

"It's seen you," Joey yelled. "It's coming in!"

Allan looked up toward the great bird. It wheeled around and dove toward them. He whipped out his sword and held it up defensively. Jill grabbed her bow and nocked an arrow. She drew back the bowstring and let the arrow fly. It struck the crefus's wing, but didn't slow it at all. Joey drew his sword and rushed to Allan's defense, but the wet ground sucked around his feet, slowing his pace.

An arrow whizzed by and struck the crefus in the other wing, this time from Peetur's bow. Still the crefus did not halt its attack. It reached out its claws and clamped them down on Emily's shoulders. Emily began to rise in the air. Allan grabbed onto Emily's legs, determined to keep her close to the ground. His feet lifted.

Joey watched helplessly from below. "Shoot it again, Jill! Peetur, save them!"

A barrage of arrows bombarded the bird. It shrieked again as it dropped from the sky and landed on top of Allan and Emily. The crefus shuddered, then was still.

Joey, Jill, and Peetur ran forward and began pushing the giant bird. After an agonizing minute, the crefus rolled away. Allan sat up.

"I'm alright," he said. "Emily, are you okay?"

"As okay as anyone can be after being almost carried off by a freakishly large bird," she said grumpily. "But I'm alive."

"Why aren't they hurt?" Joey asked. "I should think it'd be worse than that."

"Ye are Time Captives," Peetur said. "Ye canna change, which means ye canna be hurt."

"Hey, Jill, maybe you can't get any mosquito bites, after all," Joey said.

"Maybe," Jill conceded.

Allan and Emily stood up.

"I suppose there's nothing for it but to go now," Allan said.

Emily groaned.

"You want to face another crefus alone?" Joey asked.

"No."

"Well, then."

Peetur led the way into the marsh, the Hubbards following. Emily pouted, but she kept silent. Jill held tight to Allan's hand seemingly desperate for comfort and support. Joey glanced back at Emily, but didn't offer her any assistance. She'd just refuse it if he did.

Peetur and the four children trudged through the marsh, hour after hour. They had given up trying to speak to one another. It was quite enough to find relatively solid ground to step on, then pull one's feet up out of the inevitable mud.

Joey's feet were soaked through. He didn't mind being wet, he loved wading in the creek at Creighton Hill, but three hours of trudging through marshland was pushing it a bit.

Emily stumbled along behind him, muttering complaints under her breath. Joey would have done the same had he not been determined to be as opposite of Emily as possible. It was the only way he could bear it any longer. At least he wasn't getting eaten alive by mosquitoes.

He scanned the distant horizon. The sun was setting ahead of them, though they were heading south. It was a peculiarity of this new world. But before the sunset was a lake.

"There's the end of the marsh!" Joey cried out.

This knowledge gave the children a new burst of strength. They hurried onward at an increased pace. The ground solidified a bit. Joey no longer had to fight against thick mud with every step. Finally, they emerged from the reeds onto the beach of the lake.

Jill heaved a sigh of relief. "We made it."

"Aye," said Peetur. "We'll camp here tonight."

Even Emily was too tired to protest sleeping out in the open.

CHAPTER FOURTEEN
THE ATTACK

1865

ABIGAIL TRIPPED LIGHTLY THROUGH THE BED of flowers, gathering a bouquet of sweet summer blossoms. Luuke's granddaughter Ammeelia was to be married today and it had fallen on Abigail to gather her bridal bouquet. Dear Ammeelia, who was like a little sister, or niece, or something of that sort to her.

It had been more than forty years since Abigail had arrived in the kalican village, and she had seen two generations grow up. Yet she herself still was to all appearances twelve years old. She had often struggled with her status as a Time Captive, particularly when word had come of others imprisoned at Crannig Castle. Through it all, Luuke and Evalin had been there for her, helping her cope with her unchanging state.

Staying twelve was not entirely unpleasant. She didn't have to undergo the difficulties of growing up. However, she often longed to change. It was dreary to be the same day after day.

She was dwelling too much on herself. This was Ammeelia's special day. She must have a beautiful bouquet for it. The green stems of flowers stained her fingers slightly, and gave them an odor of the freshness of spring. It was such a beautiful day. Just perfect for a wedding.

The bouquet seemed to be large enough. She sat down on the grass to arrange the flowers. The blooms looked lovely together. She wrapped a strip of brightly colored cloth around the stems and tied it into a bow. Perfect.

A distant pounding drew her attention. She scanned the horizon in the direction of the sound. It came from the east, never good news. Only Calhortz lay to the east. A group of horsemen appeared. The riders were tall and thin, pale even, though she could not see much more at that distance. Still, it could mean only one thing. Strytes.

The bridal bouquet was forgotten in a moment of instant terror. Abigail jumped to her feet, dropping the flowers as she did so. Her one thought was to reach the village and warn her adoptive family. She lifted her skirt and ran for the village. The wigwams grew closer and she began to hear the happy laughter that accompanied such a joyous occasion. Was it all to be for naught?

"Luuke!" she cried. "Roobin! Come quickly! There are strytes approaching the village!"

Roobin hurried towards her. It was not often Abigail behaved in such an unladylike manner. "Are ye sure?"

"Yes." Abigail's voice was full of fearful tears. "Oh, Roobin, I'm so frightened. What will they do to the village? What will they do if they discover I am a Time Captive?"

Roobin didn't answer. He looked toward the east, toward the approaching strytes. His face took on a worried expression. "Men! We have an approaching attack."

The laughter and merriment ceased. What had only moments before been a scene of revelry and rejoicing, quickly became a place of defense. Abigail sought out Evalin, Ammeelia and the rest of the women of the family. She must be with them in such a time. They needed her, and she needed them.

The strytes drew nearer. There was no longer any doubt who they were, or that their intention was of no good. They were fierce people, well-armed, a war party out for blood. The kalican men met them outside the village as the women and children hid inside. Abigail knew they would try to negotiate peace, just as she knew it would be fruitless. The subsequent screams of agony were evidence she was not wrong.

The smell of smoke wafted into the wigwam in which she was hiding. However, this was no ordinary cook fire smoke. It carried a strange quality to it. The wigwams were burning.

"Quickly! Get out!" she cried. "We shall be burned alive!"

Abigail grabbed the bow she had taken from the attic back home and slung the quiver over her shoulder. They rushed out into chaos. Smoke and flames rose around the village. Women and children ran about, trying to save what they could. The strytes walked among the wigwams, swords drawn. Abigail stood a moment, watching them in a horrified trance.

The strytes were torching their homes. Through the smoke, Abigail caught a glimpse of the village outskirts. It was littered with bodies. The men were all dead.

Abigail suddenly felt faint. Screams rose around her. She realized with horror that the men were not the only ones to be slaughtered by the strytes. This couldn't be happening.

An all too familiar scream echoed behind her.

Abigail whipped around.

"Ammeelia!" The kalican girl sank down to the ground. Red stained the front of her white dress, spread across a wide slash. Abigail darted forward and cradled Ammeelia in her arms. Ammeelia's face was white and drawn, creasing with intense pain.

"No, Ammeelia, no." Tears coursed down Abigail's face. Ammeelia was so young, her whole life before her. She was to be married that day. Now . . .

"I won't let this happen to you," Abigail said. "Just hold on. You will be fine."

"Abigail," Ammeelia breathed. Her countenance turned to terror as her gaze shifted past Abigail. "Abby . . ."

Abigail looked up. A stryte stood over her, his bloody sword raised. Panic overtook her. Her heart pounded frantically. Time seemed to slow as his sword came down. She gathered Ammeelia close to her and shielded her from the impact. She expected any moment to be dealt her deathblow. The stryte's sword glanced off her head.

She chanced a glance up at the stryte. He gave her a queer look, then shouted something Abigail could not discern to the other strytes. A moment later, he grabbed her arms and hauled her to her feet. Abigail fought to retain her hold on Ammeelia, but it was beyond her strength. Ammeelia slipped to the ground with a groan and a whimper. It nearly broke Abigail's heart to hear it. The stryte wrested her bow from her grip and pulled away her quiver of arrows. Abigail didn't have the heart to struggle.

The stryte dragged her along to his horse and threw her upon it. He swung himself up behind her. All around, the strytes mounted their horses. As they rode away, Abigail looked for the last time at the village that had long been her home. Tears streamed down her face as she took in the sight of burning wigwams and bodies strewn about. And as a Time Captive, she couldn't even share their fate.

She set her face forward and prepared for an even more terrible future.

~

The castle walls loomed high around her. She truly was a captive now, even more so than being a captive of time. She had lived so long without walls that they seemed stifling, despite the high arch of the ceiling. She stared at the ornate doors before her and took a deep breath. She would be in the audience of Mudan, king of Calhortz, and Toarna his queen in a matter of seconds.

The guard next to the door gave her a reassuring smile, then pushed the door open. Abigail stepped forward. The ceiling was even higher than the one in the corridor. The walls were hung with tapestries, and lighted torches were mounted about the room to supplement the little light that came through the narrow windows. At the far end of the room sat Mudan and Toarna.

She crept forward, not daring to look them in the eye, for fear they should sentence her to an even worse fate.

"Are you the Time Captive that was captured in the land of Kalica?"

Abigail raised her eyes slightly, but still did not look at the king's face. "Yes, Your Majesty." *The only one to escape the massive slaughter.*

"Very well, then," King Mudan said. "You will be pleased to know that you are no longer alone. You are one of four Time Captives now. You will be sent for study along with the others to the Tower. You will also be expected to do certain tasks about the castle. Is that understood?"

"Yes, Your Majesty."

"Owen, take her to the Tower."

The guard from the door entered the room. "Come with me."

Abigail turned away from the king and queen and followed. She didn't dare speak to the guard, though he seemed kind. Finally, he paused and opened a door. He stood to the side to allow her to pass. She stepped forward.

"I am on your side," he whispered.

She looked quizzically at him. He did not explain.

"Go." The dark staircase through the door did not look at all appealing.

Abigail took a fleeting glance at Owen, and then stepped inside. He may have been on her side, but that did not make walking into the dark unknown any better or easier. If anything, it made it worse. She ascended the stairs.

Halfway up she began to hear voices. Happy and frolicking voices.

She pushed open the door at the top of the stairs. Light spilled into the stairway. She stepped in hesitantly. Three children were gathered around an elf seated at a table, bent over a piece of paper. Abigail tiptoed forward, not wishing to disturb them. She walked around the table and looked at the paper. One of the boys was drawing on it in ink, a poor drawing of a stryte, but quite a funny one. The stryte in the drawing wore a dunce cap, and had a bucket of water being poured over him.

The girl giggled. "It's not quite like him."

"If it isn't, no one can get in trouble for it," the other boy said.

The elf nodded. "Very true."

The boy who had been drawing the picture looked up. "Hello. We were told there was a new

Time Captive coming. Are you she?"

"Yes. I am Abigail."

The children looked at each other.

"She is a Time Captive indeed," the girl said. "My great aunt. My name is Mary. It is good to finally meet you."

"I am George," the boy who had drawn the picture said. "This is Thomas," indicating the other boy, "and this is Camthalion," indicating the elf.

"I am your brother Noah's son," Thomas said. "Mary is my brother John's daughter."

Abigail looked toward George. "I suppose, then, you are the brother of my father Josiah."

"Yes," George said. "You look very much like Priscilla Ames. Is she your mother?"

Abigail nodded. "Then we are family."

"That is so," George said. "Being Time Captives appears to be a family affair."

Chapter Fifteen

A Fishing Boat and a Violin

2000

"Joey, wake up. It's morning."

He opened his eyes to see Allan above him. The sky was barely turning pink. He sat up.

"I'm still wet."

"Tell me about it," Emily said. "Sleeping outside is the most miserable thing ever. Worse even than that wretched wigwam."

Joey glanced at Peetur. He was handling the insult far better than Joey would have done. His drawn mouth was the only indication he had heard and not appreciated this comment.

"Can I help with the fire?" Joey asked.

"Aye," Peetur said.

"How?" Joey asked. "I've never un-banked a fire before."

"You never banked one before either," Emily said.

Joey decided to ignore her.

"Move the logs apart," Peetur instructed. "Then add brush to it."

Joey did as Peetur had directed. The fire leapt to life. "Look!" he exclaimed. "I'm better than a Boy Scout."

"Right," said Emily. "What's for breakfast?"

Jill rummaged through her pack. "We have bread and dried meat."

"Ugh. That's what we had yesterday."

"I don't see you catching any fish," Joey said. He didn't want bread and dried meat for breakfast any more than Emily, but he didn't want Peetur to think he was a complainer. He was, but nobody had to know that.

Jill passed out chunks of bread. Peetur said a blessing and they ate their breakfast.

"Are we finding a way to cross the lake, or will we go around?" Jill asked.

"We could build a raft," Joey said. "I've always wanted to do that."

"Yeah, and have it sink as soon as we get on it," Emily said.

"We will have to cross a river whether we cross the lake or not," Peetur said. "The River Everlong is between us and Calhortz."

Jill shuddered. "I'm afraid to go into Calhortz. If only half of what you told us about strytes is true, we won't survive."

"Remember the crefus, Jill," Allan said. "We are Time Captives. And even if we are not, still we cannot die unless it is God's time."

"Yeah, and you remember what Naythin said about the attack that wiped out the whole village one hundred and thirty five years ago," Joey said. "The strytes come here too."

"Aye," Peetur agreed.

"I still don't get how there are still kalicans when the strytes wiped them out," Emily said.

"A few survived," Peetur said. "Those few re-built our race, time and time again."

"So you lied about getting wiped out." Emily rolled her eyes and turned her attention away from the group.

"They didn't," Joey protested. It wasn't fair of Emily to say so.

"Hey, there's a boat out there, if any of you blind people care," Emily said.

Joey squinted at the lake. He wasn't blind, not by a long shot. It wasn't fair of Emily to say so. "Hey, there *is* a boat."

The boat was a rather large fishing vessel and it was heading roughly in their direction.

"What country owns this lake?" Allan asked. "Do you think it's an enemy?"

"I should be surprised if it was from Calhortz," Peetur said. "Briznom owns this area. They keep mainly to themselves, but they are generally friendly to my people."

Joey jumped up and began waving his arms around and shouting.

"What are you doing?" Emily demanded.

"Getting us a ride," Joey said.

"Good idea." Allan too began jumping about and waving his arms.

"You two look ridiculous." Emily folded her arms contemptuously.

"If it saves us some walking." Jill joined her brothers.

"Make fools of yourselves if you must, but don't drag me into it," Emily said.

"We've been seen!" Joey cried. Men looked toward them over the side of the boat. They pointed at the Hubbards. "We've got to get to them."

"Are you kidding? Do you know what that would do to my nails?" Emily said.

Joey didn't heed her. He waded into the lake and began swimming toward the fishing boat. He was a strong swimmer, but still he was tired by the time he began to near the boat. He floated on his back to rest. A rope landed in the water near him.

"Hold onto the rope and we'll pull you aboard," one of the fishermen shouted to him. Joey grabbed the rope. He glided effortlessly through the water by the strength of the fisherman aboard. The boat did not rise very high out of the water, so he easily scrambled aboard. He stood facing the fishermen, water dripping off him and pooling around his feet.

"What is a young boy like you doing out at the lake today?" the head fisherman asked. He didn't seem angry, only amused.

"I'm trying to find a way across it," Joey said. "You see, we came from another world, and are trying to find a way to save the Time Captives."

The fisherman instantly sobered. "The Time Captives of Crannig Castle? No one can get in there unless they are a Time Captive themselves, or a slave. Either way, you will not come out."

"That's the thing," Joey said. "We *are* Time Captives. We got the same message in the attic back home as all the others. And we want to join them. It's just my sister's a real complainer about this whole thing and the rest of us would rather not walk any more than we have to either, so we'd really appreciate a ride to the Everlong."

The big fisherman was silent for a moment. "I can take you to the mouth of the Lefner River and give you a rowboat in which to continue your journey, but I must warn you, it is no easy task to enter Calhortz undetected. Strytes patrol the border, privateers the waters. Toarna is on the lookout for Time Captives. She has come to hate and fear them."

"We've still got to go," Joey said. "Won't you please help us?"

The fisherman hesitated, then looked toward his men. "Bring the boy's friends aboard, then set our course for the Lefner River."

The men hastened to obey.

Score! Joey felt very proud of himself. He had just singlehandedly gotten them a ride across the lake. He certainly had the bragging rights for this stage of their journey.

"I'm going to be seasick," Emily declared as soon as she was brought aboard.

"You're fine," Allan assured her. "You have an iron stomach. You can ride the wildest rides at Six Flags without getting sick."

"Yeah, if anyone gets seasick it should be Jill," Joey said. "She's got the weakest stomach of all of us."

"I'm fine," Jill said. "We're only on a lake."

"True," Joey acquiesced.

"You're positive you want to go through with this," the fisherman asked Joey.

"Absolutely."

"Then we will head for the Lefner River."

"All right," Joey said. "Time Captive relatives, here we come!"

~

1865

Abigail walked dejectedly around the Tower. The book-lined walls were a bit of a comfort to her, but more than anything they reminded her of home—her real home, Creighton Hill, which she had not seen in over forty years. It did no good to keep to her bed, for she only remembered the horror of the slaughter of her friends. Besides, they were forced to appear before Mudan every day, as Camthalion reported his findings on their situation. It was nothing, really, he knew that their state could not be emulated by created beings.

At least they were not worked mercilessly. Yet she had to see the slaves who were worked to death. So many of the human and mer slaves died soon after arriving. Their value to the strytes was so little that they did not mind replacing them as soon as they arrived.

And the strytes had killed the kalicans who had become her family during her years in this world. She had to struggle against hate for them. It wasn't that hate was unladylike, it was wrong. Yet she needed something to bring her solace.

That was when she noticed the violin in the bookcase. It had been so long since she had seen one. Too long. Without hesitation, she picked it up and drew the bow across the strings. She flinched at the flat notes, and hurriedly tuned the instrument. She set her bow and played the first few notes of a Handel sonata. It was strange how, after forty five years, she still remembered it perfectly. On the other hand, perhaps it was not so strange considering that she had been frozen in time all those years.

"You play the violin?"

Abigail turned to see Camthalion. "Yes, sir."

"Toarna has been in want of a court musician for some time," he said. "I think you would do well to play the part."

"What happened to the last musician?"

"He was executed for opposing Mudan's treatment of the slaves."

Abigail shuddered. "Must I?"

Camthalion nodded. Abigail lowered the violin from her shoulder.

"It will be of good use to our cause," Camthalion told her.

~

2000

Joey lay between the rowboat and the banked campfire gazing up at the night sky. It had been a full day, helping the fishermen as they sailed across the smooth, glassy lake. The men had been very talkative—it was not often they had interested youngsters on their boat—though it wasn't exactly possible to say Emily was interested in fishing. Jill at least pretended to be.

The fishermen had also tried to talk them out of their journey to Crannig Castle. Even if the Hubbards were Time Captives, they said, it was still a bad idea. Mudan and Toarna had been eager to collect them before his death, believing them to hold the secret to endless youth, but after . . .

And there they always stopped.

"Jillie, why do you suppose Toarna doesn't want to just collect Time Captives anymore?" he whispered to his sister.

"I suppose they did something she didn't like," she said. "What it is, I don't know. Perhaps she found out about the rhyme back home that says we're supposed to defeat her."

"I bet she did," Joey said. "But don't you think they would be killed if she did? Maybe they aren't there anymore."

"Unless she can't," Jill said. "You remember the crefus."

"Yeah, but supposing she tried. That would be awful. Anyway, I wish the fishermen would of told us why she hates Time Captives so much."

"I'm sure we'll find out when we meet them."

"Won't it be strange to meet someone from 1800? Someone who's still a kid?"

"Yes. Goodnight, Joey."

"Goodnight, Jill."

CHAPTER SIXTEEN

RANNA

1865

ABIGAIL STOOD IN THE CORNER OF TOARNA'S sitting room, her fingers flying over what seemed like the hundredth piece of the day. Toarna sat at embroidery with her ladies in waiting, other ladies who seemed to have nothing better to do than to keep the queen company.

Abigail concentrated on her music. As weary as she was of it, it was more pleasant than listening to the queen and her ladies speak endlessly of needlepoint and the horrid gladiatorial games they all enjoyed so. Truthfully, Abigail had once cared for discussions on fashion, embroidery, and fancywork, but life with the kalicans had filled her head with more useful things. Still, she preferred frivolous conversation to the talk of man pitted against beast, and even against man, to satisfy the bloodlust in entertainment the strytes had.

The doorknob rattled and turned, and the door slowly swung inward. A girl stepped in, wearing the crisp, plain uniform of all the palace maids. She appeared a bit older than Abigail, though she was much younger in actuality. She was human, and her face held a deep tan as if she was quite used to the outdoors. She hurriedly dropped a deep curtsey in front of Toarna.

"Who might you be?" Toarna demanded.

"If you please, Your Majesty, I'm your new maid," she said. "My name is Ranna."

Toarna eyed her carefully. "Are you not a trifle young to be a personal maid to the queen?"

"Yes, Your Majesty, but I was all there was to be had."

"I see." Disapproval dripped from Toarna's voice. "I will forgive it once because it is your first time, but in the future you are not to come unless called."

"Yes, Your Majesty." Ranna dropped another curtsey. "You see, it's just that I wanted to be sure you knew who I was when it came time for needing me, and it's almost time for you to dress for dinner anyhow, and . . ."

"Silence!" Toarna reprimanded. Abigail's bow screeched to a halt. Toarna turned her head and waved her hand at Abigail. "Keep on. You are unchanging. You cannot be wearied."

To say truth, Abigail *was* wearied, but she obediently began moving her bow along.

"Go to my boudoir, and remain there until summoned," Toarna directed Ranna.

"Yes, Your Majesty." Ranna dropped yet another curtsey and hurried out of the room.

Five minutes later, at the end of Abigail's piece, Toarna rose from her chair. The ladies in waiting also rose. Without so much as bidding them farewell, Toarna went to her boudoir. The ladies followed suit, vacating the room.

Abigail lowered the violin. At last she could rest. Yet rest she could not, for the raised voices in the next room. Toarna railed at Ranna for her poor observance of etiquette. Ranna, apparently accustomed to a more lenient mistress, tried desperately to defend herself, but Abigail knew it would be fruitless.

Finally, the voices subsided. After a long silence, Toarna emerged, dressed elaborately for dinner. "Be here when I come back," she said, her eyes narrowed at Abigail.

"Yes, Your Majesty," Abigail replied.

Toarna hurried out of the room.

Ranna emerged, her manner as that of a frightened rabbit. She glanced furtively about the room. She started when she caught sight of Abigail.

"It's all right," Abigail assured her. "You don't have to be frightened of me. My name is Abigail. I am a slave here as well."

"Have you been here long?" Ranna asked.

"Not very," Abigail answered. "I lived with the kalicans for many years until the strytes came and killed them, then brought me here. I live in the Tower with Camthalion."

"In the Tower, with the Time Captives, miss?"

"Yes. I am one."

"Is it true you came from another world, and that you are to save us from slavery?"

"I do come from another world," Abigail conceded. "Before I came, I was instructed that there should be ten at the first and four at the last, and also that we must defeat the strytes. I cannot go home until then."

"I wish that I could go home," Ranna said mournfully. "But I have just as terrible a position as my brother. Neither of us shall live long."

"Where is your brother?"

"The Arena."

"I am so sorry."

"You needn't be," Ranna said. "He doesn't know

how to be a gladiator, and I don't know how to be a lady's maid, so we shall both soon be with the Creator."

"You are still young," Abigail protested. "You have your life ahead of you."

"None who are slaves of the strytes have their lives ahead of them. Only the fittest survive, and even they have no life of their own."

"Not even the fittest, if they do not comply," Abigail murmured. Her eyes filled with unbidden tears at the thought of the dear kalicans dead in their village. She took a deep breath. "You will have a true life, Ranna. I promise I will do all in my power to save you."

~

"It is not possible, Abigail."

"Why is it not? You know Toarna's ways better than I. She will not suffer an untrained maid to live. You are intelligent, George. I know you can find a way to rescue Ranna." Abigail's voice quivered with unshed tears. "I cannot let them kill another person." All the pain of her loss was bottled up inside.

"Abby, tell me about it."

Abigail bit her lip. "I would rather not."

"It helps to talk about things," George said. "It is more harmful to attempt to hold it all in. We all lost much in coming here, much we may never have again."

"It's more than just the loss of my family back home," Abigail said. "They killed the whole kalican village."

George led her to a seat. They were alone in the sitting room of the Tower, the others having gathered in the main room.

She remembered Ammeelia's face, etched with pain as she died, the burning wigwams . . . She shut her eyes against it. "They were my new family. I had no one, and the kalicans took me in, Luuke and Evalin. Then there was Ammeelia. She reminded me of my little sister Hope. I watched her grow up while I remained always the same. She was to be married the day the strytes attacked."

Abigail took a deep breath and blinked back tears. "The strytes killed them all. There is no one left. Now I am with actual family again, but from my uncle down to my grandniece, we are all the same age." She put her face in her hands. "We are all here at the mercy of the strytes, watching them kill off the weak and undesirable daily. I can bear it no longer."

"Abby, you are not the only one to have had a difficult time with our situation. I was a plantation slave for years, ridiculed constantly for my unchanging. I left my family on no pleasant terms. I was angry with them for not allowing me to go to sea."

"My father spoke of that," Abigail said. "He mourned your loss, but he forgave your transgressions."

"They are gone now," George said.

Abigail caught her breath sharply. Her father was dead, then. Her mother, grandparents, aunts and uncles were all gone.

"I cannot tell them I am sorry for the way I behaved. I cannot undo my actions. I must always carry my regrets."

Abigail took his hand. Perhaps in offering comfort she could gain some for herself. "There is much wrong I did both my real family and my adopted, and much good I neglected to do. I do not want to add any more regrets."

~

"I didn't think she'd last this long. For an untrained slave she's made a magnificent effort to be able to stay ladies' maid for a week."

"Have you found a suitable replacement?"

"There is a young mer woman from a nearby plantation that is a likely candidate."

"When is Ranna to be executed?"

"At dawn tomorrow. The mer woman is coming this afternoon."

Abigail clutched the violin under her arm, the strings making indentations on her arm. She gripped the neck with her other hand. She could not bear to play for Toarna with Ranna's death now so painfully near. Yet she must.

It was agony to listen to Toarna and her ladies in waiting casually discussing Ranna's pending termination.

It was with great relief and pounding heart, Abigail rushed to the Tower when her services were no longer needed.

George sat studying with Camthalion. Abigail returned the violin to its place, her body beginning to tremble. The bow clattered noisily on the strings as she dropped it clumsily from her quaking fingers. George looked up.

"What is the matter?"

Abigail straightened the bow and turned to George. Tears pooled in her eyes. "Ranna's execution is scheduled for tomorrow morning."

George closed the book he had been studying and stood up. "What do you want me to do about it?"

"Help. Try to rescue her. We can't just stand by and do nothing. A person is going to die tomorrow."

"People have been dying by Mudan's hand for almost a century," George said. "I cannot save them all."

Abigail drew in her breath. "I am not asking you to save everyone. I am asking you to save one person. Just one. If we do nothing, Ranna will die for no crime at all. We cannot change, so what can they do to us?"

"You have no concept of how miserable they could make us," George returned. "We may have a static physical state, but our emotional state does change."

Abigail couldn't argue that. Still, she couldn't let Ranna die.

"You once cared for the oppressed," Camthalion inserted.

"I still do," George insisted. "Now is not the time for revolution."

"I never said it was," Abigail said. "Please, do this for me. I will never ask anything else of you."

George sighed and an internal struggle played out on his features. "Fine. We rescue her tonight."

Chapter Seventeen
The Pirate Ship

2000

THE LITTLE BOAT GLIDED DOWN THE RIVER FOR the third morning in a row. A bit of cool air rose from the water, but it was mostly humid and stifling. Joey dipped his oar into the water and splashed it into the boat. The splatters of water felt good.

"Gross," Emily complained. "Do you know what's in that?"

"No," Joey said.

"And I don't want to," Jill added. "It feels good, and I don't want to be grossed out by thinking too deeply about it."

"Besides, you're already filthy," Joey said.

"We all are," Allan said, "and there's nothing we can do about it."

"I just had to decide not to care. That's the only way I can handle it." Jill looked dejectedly down at her dirt-streaked, tattered yellow gingham dress that had been so beloved.

Joey had to laugh at her expression. He couldn't possibly understand why someone would care like that about a dress. The only article of clothing he had ever been sad to see go was his favorite *Star Wars* T-shirt.

"The River Everlong is just ahead," Peetur announced.

Joey eagerly turned his attention to the river. It widened up ahead, and the trees lining the banks grew scarce. The current was stronger, pulling them toward the Everlong at a higher speed.

"Beware of the current," Peetur warned. "We need to cross the river, not go down it, but it will not be easy. Ye must pull on the oars with all yer might. Jill, help me to hold the rudder."

Jill moved carefully to sit beside Peetur in the stern. Joey set his gaze firmly ahead and gripped the oar. The boat shot out into the larger river. The current pulled them downstream. They fought against the current, struggling to keep the boat straight.

"Hey, I don't know if you care, but there's a

ship coming up the river!" Emily shouted.

Joey looked down the river. A ship was indeed approaching, rowed up river by dozens of men. The ship had a mast, but the sail upon it was furled, as it was not in use. A man stood in the bow of the ship. He wore black knee breeches, and a dark colored waistcoat over what must have once been a white shirt. His long, dark beard and tricorn hat gave him an altogether piratey look.

"'Tis the *Black Vengeance*," Peetur said. "Commanded by the pirate Captain Herb, in Toarna's employ."

"What do we do?" Jill asked in a panicked voice.

"There's nothing we can do," Peetur said.

Captain Herb peered over the bow of the ship, down at the little boat. Joey looked up at him with mixed awe and fear. He was looking at a real live pirate. He had never thought that could happen.

There was a shout and several men climbed down ropes into the water. They swam to the boat and grabbed hold of the children.

"Let go of me!" Emily shrieked.

Joey plunged into the water. For a moment, he was completely submerged. The water chilled his skin and weighed down his clothes. He came up spluttering. A hairy, muscular arm wrapped around him and dragged him towards the pirate ship. Emily splashed water all about in her struggles, her shrieks rising above all other sounds. He looked about for Jill. She struggled against her captor, but she evidently knew it was useless. There was no hope for escape in her eyes.

Joey began to rise from the river, into the stifling air. "What are you doing to me?" he demanded. Jill screamed. "And what are you doing to my sister?"

The big hairy man who was his captor only grunted in response. A moment later, he was on board the pirate ship. Jill came over the side next, and, as soon as she was released, she clung to Joey with all her might.

"Are you okay?" he asked.

Her lip trembled. "As well as I can be."

Emily landed on the deck, Allan and Peetur close behind. She got up with a stamp of her foot.

"Have you no consideration for a girl's appearance?" she shouted. "Do you know what that nasty water could do to my hair?"

Allan grabbed her arm to silence her. Captain Herb towered above them. Jill shrank against Joey, trembling noticeably. Joey shook himself free and placed his hand on his sword hilt.

"What business have you in these waters?" Captain Herb demanded.

"It concerns only ourselves," Allan answered.

"It concerns me," said Captain Herb. "No one is allowed on this river except by permission of the

Queen of Calhortz."

"Well, I don't care who she is, or who you are, but you're going to pay for dunking me in the river." Emily rushed at Captain Herb. A pirate roughly grabbed hold of her and held her back. She struggled. "Let go of me!"

Joey drew out his sword and ran at the pirate. "You leave my sister be. I'm the only one allowed to pick on her."

Emily stuck her tongue out at Joey. What a time to be so completely immature. Still, she must be defended. He raised his sword. A more skilled pirate opponent stepped in and knocked it out of his hand. Joey's sword clattered to the deck. He stooped to pick it up.

"Nice try." The pirate swiped it out of his reach.

"Allan, aren't you going to help me?"

Allan shook his head warningly at Joey.

"Disarm the rest of them," Captain Herb commanded. "Then lock them in the brig."

The pirates stripped the others of their weapons. Allan's face was hard and expressionless, but he passively accepted the theft of their special weapons. Joey knew he would be fighting if he thought it would be worthwhile, but still, how could he stand silently and let it happen?

"You can't take them!" Joey shouted. "They belong to us!"

"They belonged to you," Captain Herb corrected.

Jill clutched Joey's arm. "Don't," she whispered. "You'll only make things worse."

Though bristling with anger, Joey allowed himself to be forcibly led with Peetur and his siblings below deck. The pirates led them through rows of large, sweat-soaked men rowing vigorously, pushing the boat upriver. Jill shuddered as she walked through. Joey felt almost the same; the bulging muscles of the pirate sailors were not exactly comforting when they were one's enemy.

Still further down they went, the brig was in the very bowels of the ship. The air was even more damp down here, and smelled strongly of mold. Several cells lined the walls. One of the pirates unlocked two of them. The boys were shoved into one cell, the girls into a neighboring one. The pirates slammed the cell doors. They were locked in. Chuckling in a very cruel, irritating fashion, the pirates removed themselves from the brig.

"This place is the nastiest I've ever seen," Emily declared loudly. "I can't believe anyone would lock anyone in here."

"Why wouldn't you fight?" Joey demanded of Allan. "We could have taken them. Our weapons . . ."

"Still only leave two against a complete crew. We could not have taken them. Also, Captain Herb works for Toarna. Likelihood is that he'll turn us over to her. And where are we trying to go?"

"Crannig Castle."

"Exactly. He will be taking us exactly where we were trying to go on our own."

Joey sighed. He hated to concede an argument, but he knew when he had been beaten.

"Just look at my hair," Emily continued. "My nails are a mess, and my clothes are ruined. This place is filthy, and probably crawling with rats. I'm going to catch pneumonia, and then you'll be sorry for dragging me to this rotten place."

"Cut it out, Emily," Allan commanded sternly. All eyes turned to him in surprise. "I can only take so much," he said quietly.

Emily pouted and turned away, her arms crossed sulkily across her chest.

Jill turned a worried face toward her brothers. "Do you think there are rats in here?"

"Undoubtedly," Peetur said.

Tears welled up in Jill's eyes. Just like a girl to be more worried about rats than killer pirates.

"Will they kill us?" she said.

Joey sighed. She was worried about the truly worrisome things after all. She looked so scared. She didn't really seem like she was older than he was, though truly, there was only a year's difference between them. He didn't want her to be scared, not if he could do anything about it. He glanced at

Allan. He was about to speak comfort to Jill, but Joey couldn't let Allan be the only good brother.

Joey stepped forward to the bars and took his sister's hand. He felt stupid for doing it, but chivalrous at the same time. "Not if I have anything to say about it."

~

Allan woke to see a man standing in front of his cell. He had a horrid scar across the left side of his face which looked as if it had been caused by a giant claw, and wore a patch over his eye. He held a key in his hand. "Allan has been requested by the Captain."

Allan stood up.

"How does the Captain know that there is an Allan here?"

"Allan, what's going on?" Jill said sleepily.

The man with the claw mark glared at Allan. "I know who you are."

The others were up in an instant. Joey was at his brother's side. "What does he want?" he asked in a whisper.

"For me to meet with the Captain."

"Do it," Joey answered. "You might find out something important."

"I will meet with your captain," Allan said.

Claw opened the cell door. Allan stepped forward and the door slammed behind him. He looked back at his siblings, but Claw hurried him out of the room.

"What does the captain want with me?" Allan asked as Claw guided him throughout the ship.

"You will see soon enough."

A few moments later, Allan was ushered into the captain's cabin.

Captain Herb sat at a table, Allan's sword in front of him. Allan stood just inside the closed door, and willed himself not to react to anything Captain Herb might say. Herb picked up Allan's sword.

"It is a rare sword," he said. "I have seen six others like it, all with a different name on them. The names of all the male Time Captives. They came from another world, very unlike our own. You also have come from that world."

He held the sword so Allan could see the name upon it. It was his own.

"This is your sword, is it not?"

Allan was silent.

"The only place you could have gotten it is from the same place the other Time Captives got their weapons," Captain Herb said.

"I could have defeated a Time Captive," Allan said.

"Not likely." Herb set the sword back on the

table, this time closer to Allan. "The Time Captives got that name because they are stuck in time. Unable to change. They cannot die. Defeating a Time Captive would not be an easy task for a boy."

Allan held Herb's gaze steadily. Captain Herb did not blink. Allan began to waver and looked away.

"You may return to the brig," Herb instructed.

~

Allan stumbled into his cell. Claw shut the door and went back above deck.

"What happened?" Joey asked.

"Captain Herb knows we're Time Captives."

"You didn't tell him, did you?" Emily said accusingly.

"No. It is our weapons. They are unique and he has seen them before."

"Where?" Joey asked.

"He didn't say, but my guess would be at Crannig Castle, or by bringing other Time Captives there to turn them over to Toarna."

"Aye," said Peetur. "It is a very likely guess. Captain Herb is in Toarna's pay, and on the lookout for Time Captives."

The children were silent, reflecting on their position, and the likelihood they would soon be captives of Toarna themselves.

"We have some food," Joey said after a moment. "It's nasty, but it's food."

"I didn't eat any," Emily said. "It's moldy. But Jill was all goody goody and ate it anyway."

Joey handed Allan a piece of the bread. He managed to choke it down.

"What are we going to do?" Peetur asked.

"I don't think we can do anything but wait."

Chapter Eighteen

Rescue

1865

Abigail's fingers brushed the cold, stone wall. She shuddered at the damp, clammy sensation that spread through her body and hurried to catch up to George. Her uncle walked silently ahead of her, down the steps to the dungeon. Camthalion was behind her, treading more silently than a cat, the holder of the keys they had managed to swipe from the jailer.

George paused at the bottom of the stairs. Abigail bumped into him, instantly regretting her clumsiness. She was only with them because Ranna knew her; she did not want to cause their mission to fail. George slowly began the journey forward again. Abigail followed. She glanced back to be sure Camthalion was still with them.

They were in a long stone hall, damp and cold, lit by occasional torches. Doors of iron bars were scattered periodically along the walls. Abigail glanced anxiously through each in search of the one about whom the mission was. Men, women, and children huddled behind the cell doors. They were shrunken and pale under a thick layer of filth. Abigail nearly gagged on the stench that came from their cells. Yet she recognized no one.

"Do you see her yet?" George whispered.

"No." She moved to walk by George's side. She was frightened by the dungeon, indeed, more than she was of the strytes, and he was so much like her father and her brother Noah that being near him made her feel safe and protected. They continued on.

"Abigail?"

The voice from the cell before them startled Abigail out of her thoughts. "Ranna."

The girl stood at the bars of her cell looking out at her.

"What are you doing here?" Ranna asked.

"We're here to rescue you."

"How can you manage that? It must surely fail. We will all be killed."

"We must use all speed and stealth," George said. "It is dangerous, yes, but your staying here is more dangerous still."

Ranna nodded. "I should rather die trying to escape than be killed with no hope."

Camthalion stepped forward with the dungeon keys in his hand. He inserted them into the lock. It creaked as it turned, and the door swung open. Ranna dashed out into the flickering torchlight. She flung her arms around Abigail in a warm embrace. Abigail returned the hug.

"I knew you wouldn't fail me," she whispered in Abigail's ear.

Tears sprung to Abigail's eyes. "We haven't rescued you yet. Pray that we will be safe and successful."

Ranna stepped back, nodding her head. Tear tracks streaked through the grime on her face. Her lip trembled nervously. Abigail took her hand.

"Come along," George instructed.

Abigail led Ranna after her uncle.

"Wait."

Abigail and George turned to look at the elf.

Camthalion stood at another cell door. An elf maiden stood on the other side of the door, a man behind, three children about her. "It is my sister, Enelya, her husband Amras, and their children," Camthalion said. "We must save her and her family."

"Our agreement was to rescue Ranna," said George. "That is the plan. We will do nothing else."

"And why not?" Camthalion asked. "We are here anyway. We are making a rescue. We are planning for escape. I will not leave my family here."

"It is not possible," said George. "More people will attract attention. Our whole plan relies on being unnoticed."

"Long ago you would have saved them had you been given the opportunity." Without another word, Camthalion unlocked the cell door. Five elves emerged from the cell. "Now go."

George turned and resumed his lead, but Abigail could see from the stiffening of his shoulders and the set of his jaw that he was unhappy with the shift in plans. The elves made no noise on the hard stone floor. Indeed, she would not have known by her own ears that they were there. She silently ascended the stairs after George, still leading Ranna by the hand. She glanced back at the elves. Camthalion carried the little elf girl, the rest were on foot. She set her face forward and prepared to emerge into the castle.

The door at the top of the dungeon stairs slowly swung open. George peeked out. He reached his hand back towards Abigail. She took it, and they advanced from the dungeon. She couldn't quite tell if the sweat on her palm was from herself or from George. She suspected it was from both.

Her boots made little noise on the stone floor. Indeed, her heart seemed to make more noise than her feet. She strained her eyes in the dark for a sign of Thomas and Mary. They were supposed to meet them on the way to the gate to the courtyard.

Mary's blonde hair caught the flickering torch-light of the hall. Thomas stood beside her, his hand resting on the sword Camthalion had managed to procure for him. As they passed by, George gave them a silent nod of acknowledgment. Thomas gave a curious look at the train of elves behind them. George frowned, and Mary and Thomas fell into step behind George, Abigail, and Ranna.

A quick footstep echoed from behind. Surely the elves were not so clumsy and careless. Abigail glanced behind. She gasped. "We've been seen," she whispered to George. He glanced back as well.

Several armed strytes sprinted down the hall after the Time Captives. Abigail increased her speed to match George's faster pace. Ranna's hand had become cold. Abigail's breath was short and her heart pounded even harder. George drew his sword from its sheath.

The little boy elves slowed. They were so unused to physical activity they could not hold the pace. Mary took their hands and hurried them forward. The older urged his brother on.

"Come on, Draewin. We must get out." The little boy was doing all he could himself. The door to the courtyard grew larger in Abigail's sight. A stryte stood to either side, swords drawn.

"Halt!" came a voice from behind. George pulled harder on Abigail's hand. Ranna slipped out of her grasp.

"Ranna!"

Amras grabbed the girl and kept her moving toward the door. The strytes at the door rushed towards the Time Captives and their companions. George released Abigail's hand and, with Thomas, ran to meet them. They quickly dispatched the guards. George pushed the door open.

"Hurry!" Just as Mary and the two elf boys emerged into the courtyard, George and Thomas swung the heavy doors inward blocking the pursuing strytes. They sprinted across the courtyard after the girls and elves.

A clamorous commotion came from inside the castle. The gates burst open and a group of armed strytes came forth, headed by none other than King Mudan himself. Abigail was backed against the portcullis. The outside was right there. She could almost taste freedom. Almost.

Camthalion handed her the little girl and joined George, Thomas, and Amras in raising the portcullis. It began to rise, slowly. The strytes in the courtyard advanced. No. Not again. She couldn't watch those she cared about be slaughtered by the strytes. There was no way she could bear such pain again.

"The strytes are about to attack!" she yelled to them.

George, Thomas, and Camthalion turned from the portcullis and moved in front of the women, swords drawn. Abigail hugged the elf girl tighter.

"Your escape attempt will be futile," Mudan shouted. "You will not succeed, and you will suffer more than you can possibly imagine for your attempt."

"Not if I have anything to say about it," George said.

They ran to meet their enemy in battle.

"Enelya, help me," Amras said anxiously to his wife.

She went to his side, calling to her boys as she did so. "Havilan, Draewin, we must lift the portcullis."

Ranna shook with fear. Mary wrapped her arm around Ranna's shoulders.

"I'm scared," the little girl whispered to Abigail.

"Whatever happens is God's will," she said, to assure herself just as much as the child. The portcullis creaked behind them. Abigail glanced back to see the crisscross bars rise in the air.

The clash of swords filled the air. Felled strytes

were scattered about the courtyard. The Time Captive weapons did well, but not well enough. The fight drew closer to the gate. George, Thomas and Camthalion struggled to hold them back. Abigail could barely see the boys, so surrounded were they by the stryte guard. They would never be able to get away.

"Camthalion!" Amras shouted. "It's open!"

Camthalion dashed away from the fray and caught up the little girl from Abigail's arms. "We are getting out of here, Estranna."

The little girl nodded, fearful tears still pooling in her eyes. Ranna followed Camthalion through the gate, Amras, Enelya, and the boys ahead of them.

But George and Thomas still fought the strytes.

"George!" she called to him.

A scream rose up from the middle of the fight.

"My king!"

The clashing ceased. The crowd parted to reveal King Mudan. He sank to the ground in the midst of his men, a wound in his chest bleeding profusely.

Abigail looked to George. He stood beside Mudan holding his sword. Had he been the one to kill him? Mary slipped her cold hand into Abigail's.

"Should we follow?"

"Not without George and Thomas."

George looked back at the girls, his sword

dripping with blood. Abigail fought the urge to be sick. She couldn't bear the death. Not with Ammeelia's death still so fresh in her mind.

"Go!" He meant for them to leave. She was frozen to the spot. He turned and ran to them, calling to Thomas as he ran. He grabbed Abigail's arm and turned the girls toward the door. Abigail was surprised to feel her feet moving.

She was startled by rough hands taking hold of her shoulders. Her feet rose in the air. She screamed. The air felt close about her, thick and sickening. Her feet hit the ground, then her eyes found King Mudan. His countenance was filled with pure loathing. Loathing for her and her family. His mouth worked to force out words.

"You will suffer for what you have done," he spat. "Never shall Calhortz forget that you have attempted to bring destruction upon it. You may have ended my life, but rest assured, Toarna will end yours."

Chapter Nineteen
Toarna

2000

Claw appeared in the brig, several more pirates after him. Joey jumped to his feet.

"We're in Calhortz," Claw said. "Yer to be taken to Toarna."

"Great," Joey said. "Taken to our worst enemy."

"What else do you expect from a pirate?" Emily said.

Joey raised his eyebrows. Emily was accepting that they were captives on a pirate ship? She must have decided that the whole adventure wasn't a dream, though he still doubted whether she was willing to fulfill their duty.

"You'll shut yer traps." Claw stepped forward with a bunch of keys in his hand. The other pirates held five sets of manacles. Claw inserted the key into the lock. Joey slipped through the door as soon as the opening was wide enough to admit him. Allan and Peetur were close behind.

"Put yer hands behind yer back," one of the pirates demanded. Joey reluctantly did as he was told. Cold iron manacles clapped around his wrists. His hands dropped with the weight when the pirate released them. Allan was next.

"You won't put these on the girls, will you?" he asked.

"It's the captain's orders," Claw said, shutting the door of the other cell after the girls. The heavy manacles encircled their wrists and weighed them down. It appeared to be harder on them than it was for Joey.

"Are you not men?" Allan asked. "How can true men treat women so horridly?"

"Seriously, Allan, they're pirates," Emily said.

"That doesn't matter," Joey said. "Those are my sisters and you're not putting them in chains."

"Joey, you'll only make things worse," Jill said.

He didn't care. He was tired of being pushed around. He was sick of pirates. Pulling hard at the manacles, he rushed towards the man holding the girls. He got no further than two steps before a pirate grabbed his arms and twisted them painfully.

"Don't try that again," a gravelly voice spoke in his ear. His breath smelled horrid, too.

"Now take them above," Claw ordered. The fresh air would have made Joey happier had he and his brother and sisters not been in chains. The pirates led them to the gangplank. They met Captain Herb at the bottom.

"Bring them to the castle." Captain Herb barely looked at the Hubbards before he turned toward the castle and led the way thither.

The castle loomed ahead of them. It had many towers and turrets that rose high in the air. Fog rose around the castle wall. The green grass surrounding it was interrupted by a hard packed dirt road that led to the open gate, where two guards stood by the gate. Captain Herb strode confidently past them, his entourage of pirates and Time Captives of no more notice to the guards than he.

The courtyard was covered in stone. Stone walls, stone floor, a stone well in the center . . . hard and tall. It suited what Joey had heard of the strytes.

Captain Herb led them through the castle too quickly for them to notice anything but the vast size of the place. Finally, he stopped before a pair of double doors, guarded by two men in full suits of armor. The guards pushed open the doors and Captain Herb entered. Peetur and the Hubbards were hauled in and the doors shut after them. Joey looked to the front of the room. They were in the presence of Toarna.

"And what, Captain Jeremy Herb, have you brought me this time?" A woman, dressed in rich, regal robes, sat in a large, golden throne at the front of the room. Her pale face and ebony black hair contrasted sharply with her crimson gown. Her yellow eyes narrowed towards the children, and her thin lips were set in a hard, cruel line.

"A kalican and four Time Captives, m'lady." Captain Herb licked his lips nervously. Strange that a hard, callous pirate would quail before a woman, even if she was a queen and a stryte. "We captured them on the Everlong. They had come from the direction of Kalica bearing these." He motioned to his men, and two of them came forward bearing the Hubbards' weapons.

Toarna stood up and glided forward to examine them. She gingerly brushed one of the swords with her fingertips. "Allan," she whispered, "and Joey," as she glanced at the other sword. She turned to the girls' weapons. "Emily and Jill."

She turned back to her throne, her gown sweeping the floor. She sat down daintily, the crimson train resembling a pool of blood at her feet. Was it? Did she have blood on her hands symbolized by the color of her garb? Or was it because someone had been killed by an enemy? Joey supposed it could have no meaning at all, but he had been around Emily too long not to know that some girls have a reason for the way they dress.

"You are the Time Captives," Toarna said half in assertion, half in inquiry. Joey glanced at Allan. His brother had drawn himself up tall and regal, but his mouth was firmly closed.

"How did you come by your weapons? And where?"

"We found them," Joey retorted. It was true.

"Where did you find them?" Toarna's voice had lowered threateningly.

"I don't think it's wise for us to answer that, Your Majesty," Allan replied.

"Are these your names inscribed upon them?"

Allan was silent. Toarna rose from her seat.

"Oh, what does it matter if she knows our names? She already figured out we're Time Captives," Emily said.

Joey was too surprised by Emily's acceptance of being Time Captives to realize at first that she had just given them away. Allan hadn't.

"Emily!"

Toarna looked down at them, a mask of mercy superimposed over her vengeful countenance. "Say that you are not, and you shall go free."

Joey knew Allan could not deny the truth, now it was out in the open. He was too honorable for that.

"I cannot," Allan said, "for it would not be the truth."

"Swear it, boy, and you will be set free unharmed."

Allan raised his head to look squarely at Toarna and said nothing. Joey knew by the set of his jaw that he was determined not to give in.

"Are the names upon the weapons yours?"

Joey glared fiercely at Emily, but he had no need. She was just as determined as the others not to lie.

Toarna withdrew a dagger from the folds of her gown. She pointed it at Allan. "If I am not answered, you will feel the prick of this dagger and nothing else afterward. You and your brother and sisters."

"Don't worry about any of us, Allan," Joey said. After all, the crefus incident hadn't caused any injuries. Allan didn't need any prompting. Toarna hadn't needed any either.

She drew back her arm and hurled the dagger at Allan. Jill let out a shriek. Allan stood tall, bracing himself for impact. The dagger flew with deadly accuracy toward Allan's chest. The impact drove him backwards, knocking into the pirate captor behind him. The dagger clattered to the ground. Allan looked down at his chest. He was unharmed.

"In the dungeon!" Toarna shrieked. "Throw them in with the other Time Captives."

"Aye, Your Majesty," Captain Herb said. The pirates hauled Peetur and the Hubbards out of the throne room.

Toarna took Allan's sword from the pirate holding it and drew it from its sheath. The name "Allan Hubbard" was etched on the blade in flowing script. She held it up before her. The blade shone brilliantly as sunlight reflected off it. Toarna released the hilt and the sword fell to the ground with a clang. She turned to a guard. "Remove these weapons from my sight," she ordered. "You know where to place them."

"Yes, Your Majesty." The guard bowed, took the weapons, and left the room.

"You may leave as well." It was not a suggestion. The remaining pirates quickly followed suit.

Toarna paced the floor. "Time Captives," she ranted. "All of them have come. 'Ten at the first and four at the last' they say." She stopped in the middle of the floor and looked to a painting of Mudan that hung on the wall. "They shall suffer for what they have done. No matter what protection they are under, I will destroy them."

Chapter Twenty
The Execution

1865

Abigail looked up at Toarna, quaking in her shoes. Her wrists were encased in heavy manacles behind her back, and chained to the others. George and Mary stood on either side of her, Thomas on Mary's other side. Strytes surrounded them on every side. She was a dangerous criminal—for saving Ranna from death.

Toarna's yellow eyes glared down at Abigail. Her court violinist was now her enemy. Abigail felt a bit relieved at that, but she was frightened for her future.

A stryte in regal robes stood before Toarna, a

scroll in his hands. It contained their charges. Once read, Toarna would pronounce judgment. None of the Time Captives had any hope of reprieve. They had rescued important prisoners and killed Mudan, none of which would gain them any favor in Toarna's sight.

The stryte with the scroll cleared his throat and began the accusations.

"These four Time Captives, having for many years enjoyed the best of conditions at Crannig Castle, and being in great favor with the most benevolent rulers, Mudan and Toarna, did transgress against all of Calhortz. They conspired to free the most dangerous of prisoners, being the family of one Camthalion, elves of Olithea and prisoners since their opposition during the great war which gained Calhortz as a possession of Chalton. Also of freeing one slave by the name of Ranna, a former maid of Toarna, sentenced to death for her incompetency and contempt for the queen and her office.

"These four Time Captives also thereby committed treason against the king. They instigated a fight in their so-called rescue, murdering individuals of inestimable value to the kingdom. Above all, their treason and transgressions culminate in this: the murderous death of our king Mudan. In light of such acts committed, they are to be submitted to the surviving wife of King Mudan and Queen of this land for their punishment."

Toarna glared at the Hubbards. Abigail wished she could sink into the floor. George's chains clanked as he reached out his hand to take hers. It was just as Noah would have done. She wished she could tell her brother how he possessed all the chivalrous qualities of their uncle. Now she never would. Rather, she would be able to tell him, but not in their own world.

"In light of such acts of treason and murder of the highest degree, the Time Captives shall be sentenced to death by beheading," Toarna declared. "So as to discourage the slaves of the country from another such display, it shall be done in the public square in the sight of all."

~

Abigail stood with her hands manacled behind her back, a stryte executioner at her side. An enormous crowd filled the town. No, it could not truly be called a crowd. Mob would be a better term, for the gross anger of the strytes. Not that she could truly blame them. The Time Captives were responsible for the death of their king. She glanced at the others. They were in the same position as she, ordered according to their arrival in Calhortea.

Toarna stood in front, a crimson gown flowing from her shoulders and pooling about her feet. Her black hair hung down her back. Abigail trembled as she watched her, dreading what she would say.

Her voice came out as hard as steel. "We have assembled you here today to witness justice being done," she began. "These Time Captives, having led a life of luxury at Crannig Castle, did rebel against us, causing the death of my husband and our king. In commemoration of his death, and so we shall never forget what these Captives did to us, I wear crimson, to symbolize the blood they shed. And for these transgressions, they shall be put to death."

The stryte grabbed Abigail's arm and forced her forward to the execution block. The others were brought forward as well. She looked out at the crowd. She was startled to see a face that didn't glare at her in anger. It belonged to a young man, a human. Now that she noticed, there were quite a few humans in the crowd, and even some merfolk. They had been forced to come, to watch what would become of those who rebelled against the strytes.

The young man's eyes met hers. They were full of sympathy. He looked away as the executioner forced her down on the execution block. The sword rose high above her. Abigail breathed a silent prayer and braced herself for the impact of the sword that would, in all likelihood, speed her on her way to be with her Savior.

"Let them meet their fate," Toarna said.

Four blades simultaneously whistled through the air. The cold steel glanced off Abigail's neck. A great gasp went up from the crowd.

"It can't be!" Toarna cried. "The execution must go on!" Again, the blade bounced back as it touched her neck. Abigail glanced up to see Toarna's great agitation.

"Take them . . . take them to the dungeon."

~

Toarna paced her bedchamber. She paused before a painting of Mudan. "I tried to avenge you," she said. "There is something about the Time Captives we cannot understand besides their unchanging. They are immortals."

"Your Majesty?"

Toarna turned to see a maid standing in the door. "What is it?" she growled irritably.

"There are rumors circulating about the kingdom." The girl was visibly trembling. "They say there are to be more Time Captives, fourteen in all, and they have come to defeat you."

"Who is saying this?"

"The townspeople. But it is just a rumor started by an elf. The butler thought you ought to know."

"Yes," said Toarna. "Tell the general of the guard I wish to see him."

The girl bobbed a curtsey. "Yes, Your Majesty." She turned to go.

Toarna's face grew paler, if that was possible. Her eyes darted nervously about the room. The Time Captives were nothing but trouble. Their immortality had been attractive to her, but the secret to it had always eluded her. They were the downfall of Mudan. They were to be her own downfall if the recent rumors were true. Camthalion had always seemed entirely ignorant about them, but she now suspected he had been simply hiding his knowledge. And she and Mudan had been too comfortable in their life to suspect anything. They had been too comfortable to keep strong security. There was danger in being comfortable in life.

"Your Majesty?" A stryte general stood just outside her door.

She went forward to meet him. "I have reason to believe the Time Captives in custody now are not the only ones there will ever be. I want the borders of this land secured and strongly defended. Use as many men and slaves as necessary."

"Yes, Your Majesty."

"You may go."

He bowed, and left her sight. Toarna heaved a big sigh and turned back to the portrait of the late king.

"I will find a way to destroy the Time Captives," she said. "The great empire you built must be preserved at all costs. Anything else would be dishonoring to your memory, and that I could not bear."

~

The Time Captives walked along the corridor of the dungeon surrounded by their stryte guard. How different it was from the last time they had been in there! The clanking of their chains attracted the attention of the other prisoners. Abigail blinked back her tears and stared at the back of George's head as he walked before her. They were to stay indefinitely in this cold, damp dungeon. She would have welcomed the Tower and her hated job of court violinist. The prospect of staying forever in the dungeon was disheartening.

"These cells are good enough." The strytes unlocked two neighboring cells. Abigail was pushed into one with Mary and the boys into the other. The doors clanged shut.

"I knew this would happen if we went forward with that rescue," George said. "Now we cannot help anyone. Not ever again."

"Not until the time comes again," Thomas said. "When our time to act comes, God will provide a way. He always does."

"It was still worth it to save lives," Mary said.

"Save lives?" George fumed. "And get betrayed. Camthalion left us. He abandoned us to our fate. I thought he was our friend, and all he did was betray that trust."

"You betrayed his by refusing the help you had promised," Abigail said.

"And that is cause to forgive his transgressions?"

Abigail looked at Thomas.

"We ought to forgive those who have transgressed against us," Thomas said. "Not seven times, but seventy times seven. It is what God would have us do."

Chapter Twenty One

The Time Captives

2000

Allan stumbled into Captain Herb on the stone steps as Claw gave him a shove.

"Watch where yer going," Captain Herb complained.

"I am very sorry, sir," Allan apologized. Claw smirked. Joey gave him a dirty look. How anyone could like pirates was beyond him.

Captain Herb's torch lit up the stone passageway that led into the dungeon. The walls and floor were grimy, even more so than the brig of the *Black Vengeance*. The whole place smelled of reeking refuse. Straight ahead was a great iron door. Off to the side was a little room, with a cot in one corner and a table to one side. A man sat at the table, eagerly devouring a meal.

"Drake!" Captain Herb boomed. The man stood up, hastily stuffing a piece of bread into his mouth. "Toarna wants these in the dungeon with the others. And be quick about it. I want to go see my wife."

Mumbling incoherently through his mouthful of bread, Drake found keys and unlocked the heavy iron door. He held it open as the pirates filed in with the children. An occasional torch lit the passage. On both sides were countless doors made of iron bars. Drake slipped past them and marched ahead of Captain Herb. The passage twisted and turned, ever going deeper into the ground. Drake stopped before one of the doors. He inserted a key into the lock and turned it. The rusty hinges creaked loudly as the door swung open. Five girls stood inside, all appearing to be twelve years old. Emily and Jill were shoved in and the door slammed shut behind them. The boys were thrown into the next cell.

"The kalican too?" Drake asked.

Captain Herb shrugged. "Toarna didn't give any special directions."

So Peetur was thrown in after Allan and Joey. Drake and the pirates turned and walked away. There was utter blackness. Jill let out a small scream.

"Don't freak out, Jill," Joey said. He knew it was

no use, though. She had freaked out in the passage at home, and even he wouldn't deny the dungeon was far worse.

Someone struck a light in the girls' cell. The light moved towards them and ignited a torch within the boys' cell. The torches were then hung on either side of the separating wall of prison bars. Two spheres of torchlight broke the dreariness of the dark dungeon. Ten children gathered in the torch-light. Jill appeared at the edge of the light in the girls' cell. Her face was pale. He couldn't see Emily.

Joey moved into the light. The boy who had handled the torch looked about Allan's age, but if he was a Time Captive, he was probably much older. His hair was dark, and his face held a solemn expression.

"Are you Hubbards?" the boy asked.

"We are," Allan answered. "Are you?"

The boy nodded. "I am George."

"Not the same George who Grampa always said disappeared in 1800," Emily said. "That would be ridiculous."

"I am, indeed," George said. "I went through the portal in the attic of Creighton Hill in 1800, and have been here ever since."

Emily looked skeptical. "Remember that Time Captives never change," Jill told her. "They must not die either. Allan wasn't killed by that dagger."

"She is right; we cannot die," the girl who had lit the first torch said. "Toarna tried to execute us. It failed."

"And who are you?" Emily asked.

"Abigail. Mary, Thomas, and George were victims of the same failed execution attempt as well." The three named nodded in agreement.

"If you say so," Emily assented reluctantly. "I s'pose the rest of you are Time Captives, too?"

"Every one," George said. "These rest are Theodore, Samantha, Calvin, Eleanor, Jonathan, and Bethany."

"Those are the names of the ones who disappeared," Jill murmured.

"So I was right about everyone going through a voice activated portal," Joey said.

"Yeah, it's quite an adventure getting here, isn't it?" Jonathan said. "And we didn't even have to be pulled by magic, or use magic rings or anything."

"No, we just had to read some dumb rhyme on the wall that trapped every one of us in another world with pirates and little pointy-ear creatures and . . ."

"Emily, I thought you were acting better about being Time Captives," Joey said. "Maybe I was wrong."

"Yeah, you were," Emily said. "I want to go home."

"We cannot go home till we've done our best," Abigail said. "We just have to accept that we can never change or go home until we do our mission."

"We can't grow old or die?" Jill wanted affirmation.

"It appears that way," George said.

"I read a book where that sort of thing happened," Jill said. "The people were so sick of living, unchanged, forever, but they couldn't stop."

"Not that ridiculous book again," Emily complained. The others ignored her.

"I think I read that book," said Bethany, "but when I read it, I never thought it would happen to me. I hope that our case will be different, that it will have an ending as well as a beginning and a middle."

"If we complete our quest," George said.

"And what is that?"

Everyone looked at Emily in surprise.

"The reason we were brought into this world," Abigail explained. "Defeat the strytes, for this is your quest, you will not go home till you've done your best."

"But why us?" Joey asked. "We're not anything special. Why were we called to do this? I mean, I know we were, but I don't get why it has to be us. Couldn't someone from this world do just as well? It caused problems in our world for all of us to disappear. Though Anna does owe me an ice cream cone," he added as an afterthought.

"It seems to be this," George said, "'For brethren, you see your calling, how that not many wise men after the flesh, not many mighty, not many noble are called. But God hath chosen the foolish things of the world to confound the wise, and God hath chosen the weak things of the world, to confound the mighty things, and vile things of the world, and things which are despised, hath God chosen, and things which are not, to bring to naught the things that are.'"

"Like with Gideon," Abigail said. "His army was small and weak, that all would know it was not by their strength, but by God's that he won."

"You're all Bible thumpers, too?" Emily said.

"And proud of it," Bethany said.

"Are we Gideon's army, then?" Jill said.

"In a way, yes," George said. He nodded to the others.

The children all reached out to take hands. It must have been a familiar ritual to the others. Emily was reluctant, but complied. All of a sudden, as they formed a complete circle, a blinding flash of light went up from them and spread through the dark, dreary dungeon. On the children's faces was a look of awe.

"Time Captives rock," Joey whispered.

"United we stand," Allan said.

"We stand together in Christ," George said.

Joey looked about the circle. "And we are the Time Captives."

The *Time Captives Trilogy* continues in

THE CROSSWAYS

PROLOGUE

A TALL, GRACEFUL ELVEN FORM STOOD IN THE center of the throne room. The earthen tones of his clothing seemed even duller than they did ordinarily among the rich décor of the room. Toarna sat on the throne, her yellow eyes looking expectantly at the elf.

"M'lady, it has been fairly well confirmed that the Redona was hidden away by the merfolk at the conclusion of the Great War instead of destroyed as was commanded. My brother has confirmed Joseph's belief to me that it was concealed at the Crossways."

"Then should the Time Captives reach the

Crossways, they cannot recover it," said Toarna. "Nor can we."

"That is very likely, m'lady," the elf said. "However the merfolk would not have concealed it without some possibility of recovery. The Time Captives will find a way and they will set the king free."

"It is true there is a mode of recovery." Toarna pressed her fingertips together in thought. "It must be recovered and destroyed as was at first intended."

"What do you propose I do?"

"Anything necessary to secure it. You have command of my privateer fleet. Use it however you have need."

"Yes, m'lady."

"Your life depends on it."

The elf hesitated. "Yes, m'lady."

"You may go."

The elf turned and left the room.

CHAPTER ONE

ADRIEL

2000

THE SHARP CRACK OF A WHIP CUT THROUGH THE air. A long, thin strip of leather sliced through the dark, tanned flesh on the boy's back. He winced and bit his lip to hold back a scream. Down came the whip, again and again, sending searing pain through every inch of the boy's body.

He strained at the ropes that bound his wrists to the whipping post. The knots held firm, he knew they would, and he also knew that to break free would result only in more severe punishment. As the lashes continued to fall, a scream threatened to break forth. He clenched his teeth together, determined to neither scream nor beg for mercy.

He caught sight of his sister's face in the crowd of slaves that were forced to watch the beating. It was for her he was being beaten, for her he was determined not to cry out. Tears streamed down her face, creating streaks through the dirt. Just when he thought he could hold in his cries no longer, the blows ceased.

"Back to work!" the man with the whip bellowed at the slaves. The slaves turned and hurried away, having no wish to subject themselves to the punishment the boy had just received. But the boy's sister lingered near. The man with the whip untied the boy's hands and left him lying crumpled on the ground. The little girl hurried to her brother.

"Oh, Adriel," she cried, "why must you always do it? I can't bear to see you hurt."

Adriel forced a smile. "What kind of a brother would I be if I didn't?"

The little girl sighed. "Let me see." She grimaced as she looked at Adriel's bloody back. "You look awful."

"I'm alright, Rae," Adriel said. He climbed wearily to his feet, not quite suppressing a groan. Lucky he was young enough they didn't whip him into a pulp, though that likely wouldn't last long at this rate. Rae took his hand.

"I love you, Adriel," Rae said.

"I love you too, Rae," Adriel replied. But his emotional state was complicated by more than just his love for his little sister. As they walked hand in hand toward the cotton field where they were forced to labor day after day, Adriel's anger and hatred for their captors mounted. Anger towards the strytes who had conquered Calhortz and enslaved its people, who had kept Adriel's family in such unsanitary and careless conditions that it was a wonder all of his parents' children had not died in infancy rather than just four. Slave owners who had sold four of Adriel's siblings and his mother away. Overseers who had forced his father to work in the hot sun when he was ill, and not even given him a proper burial when he succumbed to the conditions.

Rae must have felt how tense he was becoming, because she squeezed his hand and said anxiously, "Don't get angry." He knew he should heed Rae's warning . . . he had been punished just as often for his defiance as for defending Rae's inability to do all that was required of her. But his smarting back, his aching body, the blood running down and soaking into his pants, Rae's timid, weak little form beside him . . . it was all getting to be too much to bear.

A whip cracked in the air. "Get to work, boy!" the overseer roared. "Or do you want another whipping and no dinner?"

Glowering, Adriel dropped Rae's hand and

went to work in the cotton field. Adriel's anger simmered inside him all day long. His back was stiff and sore, and sometimes throbbed painfully, but it was no new sensation. Ever since he and Rae had been left alone, he'd been subjected to a new whipping just as soon as the last healed sufficiently. After eating the scant evening meal provided for the slaves, Adriel retired to the shack they shared with all the other orphan slaves. Adriel sat cross-legged on his blanket in the corner, and scowled at the ground.

Rae tiptoed over with a bucket of water and a small wooden bowl of salve. She knelt beside him. "Adriel, do let me clean the blood off your back," Rae begged.

Adriel still scowled at the floor. Rae dipped a rag in the water and laid it on Adriel's back.

"Ouch!" Adriel exclaimed. "That hurts, Rae."

"It's okay," Rae soothed, sounding much older than her six years. "I just have to clean it up a bit, and then I can put some of Selima's salve on it."

Adriel grumbled under his breath, but sat still as Rae cleansed the lashes. Her gentle fingers rubbed an herbal salve over his raw back and into the wounds. It stung a bit at first, but gradually the healing power of the herbs drew out the pain. Rae's soft touch on his skin felt so like their mother's. He squeezed his eyes shut. The strytes had stolen their mother from them.

"There, now," Rae said. "Don't you feel better?" Adriel turned to look at his sister. Her brown skin, deeply tanned by long hours in the sun complemented her long black hair nicely, though the hair was rather ragged at the edges. Her dress consisted only of an old feed sack with holes cut for her arms and head, and a rope knotted around her waist. Yet her brown eyes shone, reflecting a spirit very different from his own.

"Yes, Rae," he said. "I'm sorry I snapped at you."

Her face lit up with a smile. "I'm so glad you're feeling better! Here," she handed him an extra pair of pants, "change into these. The ones you're wearing are so filthy."

Though Adriel was fourteen and Rae only six, he sometimes felt as if she was older. He didn't mind. He loved his little sister, and she was the one person left to him he didn't mind obeying. Rae tucked Adriel's dirty pants against the wall, then took his hands in hers.

"Now we must pray." She closed her eyes. "Dear God, thank you for letting us live again today. Thank you for letting Adriel and me stay together. Thank you for taking care of us . . ."

Adriel watched his sister's face as she prayed. She was so earnest, so sure that God was there, that He was taking care of them. Adriel wasn't so sure anymore. If God was there, if He really cared about them, why did He let such terrible things happen? Why had He let Adriel's mother and siblings be sold away? And why did He let his father die so cruelly?

". . . and please let the promised ones come soon to set us free . . ."

The promised ones. The prophesied children from another world who would come to deliver the Calhortans from the hands of the strytes. Rae believed the prophecy. Adriel's mother had believed it as well. But if the prophecy was true, where were the promised ones? Many said the Time Captives of Crannig Castle were the promised heroes. Maybe they were, but if so, they weren't doing a very good job of freeing the people.

". . . and please bless Adriel and help him learn to control his temper. Amen." Rae opened her eyes and grinned up at Adriel.

"It's time to go to sleep, Rae," Adriel said.

"Alright." Rae settled down on her blanket and was fast asleep in moments. Adriel lay down on his stomach, his wounded back exposed to the air, his arms crossed under his head. He sighed, then slowly drifted off to sleep.

Acknowledgements

THIS HAS BEEN THE HARDEST BOOK EVER FOR me to write. That has also made it the one that requires the most acknowledgement of others, for without them, this book would not exist.

First, I want to thank my family. You put up with countless hours of complaining, many group brainstorming sessions, allowed innumerable family conversations to be dominated by *Time Captives*, believed in the story and its worth when I was ready to trash it, and never let me give up. I thank my sister Rebekah for encouraging me by telling me that it is her favorite of all my books. I thank my dad for being brutally honest about the problems with book two, confirming my suspicions that it needed a major rewrite yet again. I thank my sister Addyson for continuing to read my writing as I write it, suggesting outcomes I never would have thought of myself, and helping this story come together.

I want to especially thank my mom. Without you, this story would be an unfinished mess sitting discarded on my desk. You helped me out of writer's block and super stuck places more times than I can count. You helped me to identify the problems and find solutions, you found ways to polish it and fix it, and you listened to my complaining more than anyone. And you told me to stop posting complaints online. You have much more wisdom than I do. :)

I also want to thank my friend Destiny for checking up on my progress and always being willing to listen to me ramble about my writing. And I thank my author friend Molly for encouraging me and letting me know that I'm not the only one with writer struggles.

My very fantastic beta readers deserve a huge thank you for catching all the mistakes I missed. Ashley, James, Mrs. Whitmire, Trinity, Destiny, and especially Jaye L. Knight, thank you for your feedback and encouragement. You have made this book better than I could have possibly made it without you.

And a huge thank you to my proofreaders, Katelyn, and Lauren, for finding all the last little typos. You guys are awesome.

My violin teacher Miriam deserves mention for directing me to Spotify, which became the soundtrack provider for the writing of *Time Captives*, with its extensive collection of *Doctor Who, The Hunger Games Trilogy, The Giver,* and *Merlin.*

For these second editions of *Time Captives*, I have to give a huge shout out to Jaye L. Knight for her endless advice on cover design. There's no way I could have pulled this off without her. Thank you, thank you, thank you.

Most of all, I give thanks and glory to God for giving me the ability to write, stories to tell, and for weaving in a message of forgiveness and redemption that I did not see coming.

About the Author

Morgan Elizabeth Huneke is a homeschool graduate who lives in Georgia. She has enjoyed creating characters and writing stories since early childhood. Books have always been a big part of her life, never more so than when working at the local library. Her other interests include reading, playing and teaching piano and violin, and politics.

To learn more about Morgan and her work, visit:

www.morganhuneke.com

or

www.morganhuneke.blogspot.com

Made in the USA
Columbia, SC
20 June 2019